THE OTHER WORST-CASE
SCENARIO SURVIVAL HANDBOOK

THE OTHER WORST-CASE SCENARIO SURVIVAL HANDBOOK

A Parody

Gene Doucette

Writers Club Press
New York Lincoln Shanghai

The OTHER Worst-Case Scenario Survival Handbook
A Parody

Writers Club Press
an imprint of iUniverse, Inc.

For information address:
iUniverse, Inc.
2021 Pine Lake Road, Suite 100
Lincoln, NE 68512
www.iuniverse.com

ISBN: 0-595-26152-3

Printed in the United States of America

Contents

INTRODUCTION

You are about to read the most important book you have ever read. All of the information contained in this volume is critically important for your continued survival on this planet, to say nothing of other planets, moons, and the many near-Earth asteroids. We have gone through great pains to present to you accurate, detailed information, sometimes going so far as to open a couple of books. In a number of cases we even risked the lives of total strangers who did things for us on a dare after consuming vast quantities of beer, which we ourselves paid for. We have even pretended we are more than one person when writing the text. This is the sacrifice we have made, the fruits of which you now hold in your hands.

You should take this handbook everywhere you go, because you simply do not know when it will come in handy. You should also share it with your friends. Buy a copy for everyone you know. In fact, if you buy it for five friends tonight, something very good will happen to you. If you do not, you will be beset upon by untold misfortune. Bob Unger from Lebanon, Maine, neglected to buy copies for any of his friends, and the next day he was eaten by wolves.

Don't take that chance!

Gene Doucette, December 2002

FOREWORD

Surviving While Also Not Dying

by "Mountain" Mel Weewee

I have been a *Surviving Until Dying Eventually* instructor for thirty years. I have taught Navy SEALs, harbor seals, Marines, the Kennedys, and two generations of pandas. I've been to Paris, the Arctic Circle, the Soviet Union, Mt. Everest, Neptune (twice,) Key Largo, and Monte Carlo. I've been to Hell and back, to Narnia, Sweden, and honey, I've been to Paradise, (but I've never been to me.) I was on the beach at Normandy, served in Vietnam and the Gulf War, the Civil War, and the War of 1812.

I've learned a lot about survival in the last three centuries.

The thing to remember, in a situation in which you intend to survive is, "try not to die." It's important to keep this in mind, for I have never met a person who survived after dying, although I understand this is possible in certain rare situations involving religious figures.

—You must be ready for everything.

I have scaled Mount Everest five times. There are no harsher conditions known to man than that which exists on and near the top of our world's tallest mountain. Once, on my fourth trip (a trip I planned because I'd accidentally left my wallet at the top on my third climb) we were pinned to the side of the mountain by a horrible storm. My Sherpa even commented that he had never seen such a terrible storm. Memorably, he stated, "I have never seen such a terrible storm." Acting quickly, he pulled out a fondue set. The cheddar fondue of the Tibetan Sherpas is legendary, of course, but only rarely does one partake of it at such extreme climes, especially in the midst of such a terrible storm. I watched silently as my companion carefully assembled the lazy susan and then lit (with great difficulty) the sterno can. Rather than use the small bowl, however, the Sherpa substituted a large chafing dish. It was not until later, when he pulled the live badger from his bag that I understood why. The fondue bowl was much too small for the badger. As I watched with chagrin and amazement, the Sherpa then stunned the badger into unconsciousness with a large rock, placed him in the chafing dish, and added snow and a small quantity of his own urine.

Within half an hour, the badger was boiled and tender (it never woke up again) and the storm had abated considerably. While enjoying this unexpected and very tasty repast, I asked the Sherpa why he had done what he did. "The god of the mountain was very angry," he explained. "When the god of the mountain is angry one must sacrifice a woodland creature to appease him."

On that day, the Sherpa's quick thinking, advance planning (very advance planning, as badgers are not indigenous to the region,) and improvisational skills—remember the chafing dish—saved the day.

—You must not panic.

The lush rainforest in the Lake Victoria region of Central Africa is one of the most magnificent places on Earth. It is also one of the most dangerous. I visit this area each year with students from my Advanced Survival Techniques course, and the rainforest expedition is the equivalent of our final exam. With the help of local guides, each of us are drugged, blindfolded, bound, gagged, and dropped somewhere within the forest stark naked. The goal is to find each other, and then find our way out of the forest while living off of the land. One year we were taken captive by a band of jungle gorillas, who beat us mercilessly and then dragged us several miles before presenting us as prizes to their alpha male.

The African Gorilla is the strongest primate on the planet. Had he grown angry with any of us he could have killed us easily with one swing of his massive arm, and so it was very important that we do everything in our power to not present ourselves as a threat of any kind. Fortuitously, we were all battered, bleeding, and completely exhausted after having been worked over extensively by the expeditionary party of gorillas that had brought us to him, so the best any of us could do was crouch meekly anyway.

As I fought the urge to panic, I recalled that on one of my previous trips to the jungle, I'd befriended a small (haha) clan of pygmy warriors. Pygmies have remarkable hearing. As the giant gorilla sodomized us one by one, I began to whistle in the way the Pygmy warriors taught me. Soon, the alpha male became tired, and left us alone. In another hour, my Pygmy friends arrived, overcame the guards, and rescued us.

Thus, our survival hinged on our ability to remain calm in a very volatile situation.

—You must have a plan.

On one occasion I found myself in something of a jam. I was in Boston, and I had to get from Logan Airport to an important meeting in Cambridge in under an hour. So I rented a car.

The streets of Boston, Massachusetts, are the most perilous and convoluted streets in the world. Navigating them requires a high degree of precision, a thorough understanding of the roads, and a degree of fearlessness that most men do not have. I had not planned well. My road map was seven years old, the car I rented was twice that—and worse, a stick shift, which I had never used before—and I'd had five gin rickies on the flight over (for medicinal purposes.) It was not long before I was involved in a minor accident that I am not under liberty to discuss pending litigation.

So my plan had failed. But I had a backup plan. I had been loathe to use the subway system in Boston because it is full of disreputable people and it always smells like urine. But, left with little option, I sprinted from the accident scene (this is not an admission of guilt) and entered what is known in the local vernacular as the "Blue Line." After boarding the train—a dangerous and violent procedure—I re-examined my plan and discovered that the "Blue Line" does not go to Cambridge. Indeed, a perilous transfer would have to be undertaken. I needed to figure out a way to get to the "Red Line" but the "Red Line" did not cross the "Blue Line" at all! I could take the "Orange Line" to get to the "Red Line" or the "Green Line" to get to the "Red Line" but while the "Orange Line" and the "Green Line" both crossed the "Blue Line" and the "Red Line" they did not cross each other! Well, this was very confusing. Instinctively, I understood that confusion was my enemy. So I went to my third plan, left the subway and hailed a cab.

My cab driver was very kind. He immediately understood that I was not from these parts and promised to guide me to my destination. His bravery was staggering, and the courageous fellow would no doubt have gotten me to Cambridge in ample time given that he was driving 97 miles per hour on average. Tragically, I could not complete the journey with him as I realized I had insufficient cash to complete the journey. At a convenient slow-down on a pathway known as "Storrow Drive" I took my leave of him by leaping from the cab onto a grassy strip alongside the road.

Fortuitously, I was almost there, as I was separated only by the Charles River from the Eastern portion of Cambridge. With time of the essence, I secured my equipment and swam the river. I made it to my important meeting with five minutes to spare.

What did I learn? I had kept my head. I had recognized the flaws in my plans early on and acted without hesitation to correct them. I had to get a tetanus shot for swimming in the river. But most importantly, I had a plan, and a backup plan, and a backup to the backup plan.

This guide may help you learn, as I have, to survive, and also to not die. Although I doubt it. Frankly, the whole thing is a load of crap.

PART I

BREAKING IN AND BREAKING OUT

—How to Shoplift

—How to Rob a Bank

—How to Break Into a Car

—How to Escape from Prison

—How to Get Into Heaven

—How to Split the Atom

—How to Avoid a Speeding Ticket

HOW TO SHOPLIFT

1: <u>Wear baggy clothing</u> This is much easier to do in cooler climates. You may look suspicious wearing loose sweatpants and an overcoat in Florida. Be sure to choose a coat with inside pockets.

2: <u>Pick the right store</u> This really depends on the sort of merchandise you are interested in acquiring. Try to stick to stores that sell things that can be carried in a pocket. For instance, you will not get very far with a stereo shoved under your shirt. Likewise, pick merchandise that has at least some value. Nobody is going to be all that impressed if you steal a head of garlic. Compact discs, small electronic equipment, watches and jewelry are all very popular items.

3: <u>Check the security</u> Be sure to familiarize yourself with the security and surveillance equipment. Is there a sensor at the door? These are usually easy to find. Cameras? Most security cameras are hidden behind one-way glass or inside of darkened glass bulbs on the ceiling. Armed guard? If there is an armed guard, you're trying to take something that's too expensive. Go somewhere else.

4: <u>Misdirect</u> This is a magician's skill that comes in handy when shoplifting. (Most professional magicians don't pay for anything.) What you want to do is select the item you wish to take with you from the store. Position yourself near it, and then pick up a DIFFER-ENT item. Hold this second item up, look at it in the light, lick it if you want to, just so long as anybody watching you do this is observing your actions with this particular item. Meanwhile, your other hand is grabbing the object you actually want and slipping it into your coat pocket.

5: <u>Getting out the door</u> Sprinting to the exit at this point would be a good indication that you've done something you should not have done. Instead, walk calmly out of the building, provided there are no sensors. Otherwise, see below.

6: <u>Fooling the sensors</u> There are a great number of ways to get past the door sensors. Understand first that what the sensors are looking for are electronic tags on the merchandise. The first thing you should do before slipping your prize into your pocket is identify the security tag. Pulling it back out of your pocket to check is not recommended.

—<u>The courtesy sensor</u> This is when the sensor is not directly in front of the door, and customers are just expected to know to walk through it. Just don't walk through it. Or, if you are under surveillance, start to walk through it, and then drop your keys on the outside of the sensor. Lean over to pick them up and then walk around.

—<u>The friendly counter-person</u> Often, there is a pad near the register that deactivates security tags. Find a friendly counter-person, start up a conversation, and ask to see something behind them. Lean over to point at what you're interested in. When their back is turned, rub your pocket against the deactivation pad.

—<u>Catch the shoplifter</u> This requires some skill. What you want to do is sidle up near another customer—preferably one with a large overcoat of their own—and slip an article of merchandise into one of their pockets without them noticing. (Since they are probably also shoplifting, be careful to check your own pockets after making contact with them.) If you cannot find someone with appropriately large pockets, try and remove the security tag (most are adhesives) from something else in the store, and stick it onto the stranger's back. Then, when the stranger attempts to leave, make sure you are right behind them. The sensor will go off, of course, but you're not the one who will get arrested. As the helpful stranger is being pummelled into submission, slip out of the store.

Things to know

—Shoplifting is against the law.

—On the other hand, retail stores budget for shoplifting. The price of the merchandise is based, in part, on the assumption that some merchandise simply disappears without ever being paid for. So essentially, what you are taking has already been paid for by the friendly shoppers who have come before you.

—Shoplifting is a great way to prove to the other kids in school that you are really cool.

HOW TO ROB A BANK

When robbing a bank it is a very good idea to collect enough money to make it to a country that does not currently have an extradition treaty with the United States.

You will need: A gun

1: <u>Choose your target</u> It would be wise to select a bank branch that is not in an isolated region with only one road leading to and from the bank. A bank in a downtown locale is a pretty good spot, except that police tend to be somewhat more common there, and you will have to flee on foot. You should case out the interior of the branch carefully as well. What you want to look for is large amounts of money just lying around doing nothing. This may not be as difficult to find as you think.

2: <u>Don't bother with a mask</u> Wearing a mask or a stocking over your face may tip off the staff regarding your intentions. Instead, keep in mind that the security cameras are usually ten feet off the floor and pointed downwards. Wear a baseball cap and sunglasses, and do not look up.

3: <u>Approach a teller, and ask her for all her money</u> Try to avoid mentioning a gun, as this will look bad in court. In the unlikely event that she says "I'm sorry, but I cannot give you all of my cash until you provide me with evidence of a gun, and two forms of identification" you will have to show her the gun (but not the identification.)

4: <u>Take the cash</u> Accept only paper currency. Do not accept coins, travelers checks, or bank checks. Put the currency in the bag we neglected to mention you should have brought with you. You will not, in all likelihood, get enough cash to leave the country.

5: <u>Go to the next teller</u> Keep going down the teller line until you think you might have enough to at least rent a car and drive to the state border.

6: <u>Get out, fast</u> Hopefully, the entire local police force will not be assembled outside when you attempt to leave. (If they are, we recommend not showing them your gun either.)

7: <u>Do not open the bag right away</u> No matter how eager you are to count your take, wait for a while before doing so. People only rarely count large sums of money when standing around outside, and doing so might look suspicious. Also, give the dye pack a chance to explode while contained within the bag, so you don't get it on your clothes.

Things to know

—You will probably get caught, as this is an exceptionally bad way to obtain money that is not already yours.

—If you do get caught, we don't know you. Okay?

—Chicks dig bank robbers.

HOW TO BREAK INTO A CAR

Under certain circumstances, when you are in grave need of immediate vehicular transportation, it is necessary to gain entry to a motor vehicle that you do not have the keys to. These sorts of emergencies pop up very frequently in major metropolitan areas.

1: <u>Make sure the owner is not around</u> Often, the best way to determine this is to "stake out" the vehicle. Watch it when it is parked, and determine where the owner is going.

2: <u>See if they left the keys in the car</u> Not very likely, but that sure would make this go a lot more quickly, wouldn't it?

3: <u>Get into the car</u> If the door is left unlocked, or the window left open, just climb in. Be aware that if the door is unlocked or the window is down, this may be an indication that the owner will be returning shortly. If you have no particular qualms about damaging the car, try breaking one of the windows. Put a piece of cloth over the rear passenger side, and then strike the window with a ball peen hammer. This should create an opening large enough to enable you to reach inside and unlock a door.

4: <u>Try to hotwire the car</u> Pop the plastic off the side of the steering wheel with a screwdriver, strip a couple of wires, and then connect them together. This will not work, as the movies have been lying to us for years. But at least you tried it.

5: <u>Wait for the owner by hiding in the back seat</u> Hopefully you have thought to bring a weapon with you, or this is not going to work very well.

6: <u>Threaten the owner with the weapon</u> Make him or her drive to a secluded area and give you the keys, so you can drive to wherever it is you had to go in such a hurry.

Other Methods

—<u>Carjacking</u> Rather than hiding in the back seat, sneak up behind the owner as they get into their car. This is a good way to get the keys without having to worry about the owner's driving skill. It also requires a good hiding place somewhere near the car. Do not hide under the car. This is just stupid.

—<u>The Fake Valet</u> Get hired as a valet for a restaurant. If you stand outside the restaurant wearing your ugly valet jacket, people will actually HAND you their keys. Really.

—<u>Commandeering</u> This is actually very similar to carjacking, except that you are either a police officer or have one of their badges (available on the internet.) Run up to any car, flash the badge, and announce "Official police business. I need to commandeer this vehicle." We have always wanted to try this ourselves.

HOW TO ESCAPE FROM PRISON

Prisons vary widely in size and design. Some have a minimum of guards, little in the way of restraining walls, and only token barbed wire. Others have nearly as many guards as prisoners, several walls, barbed wire, razor wire, minefields, sharpshooters in towers, and are located on remote islands. Often, the prison you are assigned to (you do not usually get to pick one yourself) is dependent upon the crime you have actually committed which resulted in your incarceration. For instance, if you have stolen a car, *(See "How To Break Into A Car")* you might find yourself in a fairly lax prison. If you have robbed a bank at gunpoint *(See "How To Rob A Bank")* you could end up in a maximum security facility, especially if you actually shot someone while robbing the bank. If you do not know the details of the prison you are being sent to, ask around. Many police officers can be very forthcoming regarding this information.

You will need: A spoon, and a tremendous amount of free time.

1: <u>Find a weak spot in the wall of your cell</u> By federal law, every prison cell has a spot somewhere in it where the cement is crumbling due to water damage or termites or something. In brand new prisons, old cement is actually imported.

2: <u>Chip away during the night</u> Use the spoon to open up a hole in the wall. During the day, put your bed in the spot, and carry the old cement pieces out to the yard in your pockets. Do not eat the loose cement pieces thinking this will save time.

3: <u>Find out what's on the other side of the hole</u> With any luck whatsoever, the hole will lead to some sort of space between the cell walls, and with a little more luck that space will be large enough for you to fit into. If the hole just leads to the cell next to you, you've got a problem.

4: <u>Build a dummy</u> Put a dummy in your bed so that nobody notices you're not in it. A mannequin would be ideal, but difficult to get your hands on. In a pinch, a full laundry bag might do the trick, provided you usually sleep in the fetal position.

5: <u>Sneak into the opening</u> It will take some time for you to find out where the space between the walls leads, so you may want to rely on others for assistance. There should be at least two or three fellow prisoners in there on any given night, especially if they have read this book. Ask them.

6: <u>Start digging again</u> If you are fortunate enough to be within a wall that has an opening that leads outside, rejoice heartily (but quietly.) You are not free yet, but you have at least been spared the trouble of having to chip away at another wall. Now you're going to have to dig a tunnel. The ideal tunnel should be no fewer than ten feet deep in order to get below the outer wall, and also to prevent it from collapsing in on itself. With a spoon, this should take no more than ten to fifteen years.

HOW TO GET INTO HEAVEN

There are many different religious opinions regarding the best way to ensure getting into heaven. What follows is a synthesis of some of the more popular approaches.

1: <u>Get born into a Brahman household</u> The Hindu caste system is very explicit on this. You're not going anywhere special in your next life if you're born into a lower caste.

2: <u>Get baptized</u> Wash away that original sin.

3: <u>Get circumsized</u> (Men only)

4: <u>Have a Bar or Bat Mitzvah, first communion, and confirmation</u> It may be possible to do all of this in one weekend. Ask around.

5: <u>Do not reveal any part of your body—even your face—to any man except your husband</u> (Women only)

6: <u>Do not be a homosexual</u> Most major religions are pretty clear on this, although if this is unavoidable, there may still be an opening in the priesthood.

7: <u>Don't kill anyone who believes in the same thing you do</u> "Don't kill anyone" would seem to be a much simpler directive, but it is inaccurate. Muslims are allowed to kill infidels, Catholics are permitted to kill Jews and Muslims, Jews are welcome to kill Muslims and the occasional Catholic and, just to confuse matters, it's okay for Protestants and Roman Catholics to kill each other in some parts of the world. As this is very confusing, you may wish to adopt the standard practice of asking someone you're about to kill what their religious leanings are before you kill them.

8: <u>Read the books</u> Adhere closely to the teachings of the Bible, the Koran, the Torah, the book of Mormon, the Baghavad Gita, and the teachings of Confucius and Lao-Tse. (As of this printing, the Buddha had not yet submitted an official manuscript due to excess bliss.) Resolve contradictions between the books with a coin flip. Resolve contradictions within each book with a coin flip as well.

9: <u>Do not have premarital sex</u> You may have to marry everyone you wish to have sex with, but don't worry; according to several religions, it's okay to do this.

10: <u>Don't speak the lord's name in vain</u> Especially Allah. This will get you in a LOT of trouble. If you use it, really mean it.

11: <u>Don't eat pork</u> A couple of religions have real issues with pigs. Nobody knows why.

12: <u>Do whatever a deity asks</u> Deities pop up every now and then and ask people to do strange, irrational things, like sacrifice children or give away all their money to charity, shave their heads and wear orange robes. It is very important that you do this but first, make sure it's really a deity doing the talking. If, for instance, someone is telling you they got this info directly from a god of some sort, check their references first.

13: <u>Get last rites</u> This should happen before you actually die. If possible, hang out a lot with priests and rabbis just in case.

Things to know

If you are still uncertain regarding your odds on getting into heaven, do some research. Some evangelists offer specials whereby for a small sum of money, you can buy a spot in heaven. Many also offer package deals.

HOW TO SPLIT THE ATOM

In today's political climate, it is wise to seriously consider developing nuclear capabilities. If you are a small nation-state, having the bomb can be very useful in negotiations, and many households in the United States already employ nuclear weaponry for home security.

1: <u>Choosing the right atom</u> It would be a mistake to assume that any old atom will do. Theoretically, this is true, but practically speaking, you will have a good deal of trouble splitting smaller atoms, such as oxygen. Instead, you are going to have to find a large atom. Your best choices are uranium or plutonium. We recommend uranium, as you will find that it is much easier to come by. Uranium is a naturally occurring element that can be mined, and is also available now in many specialty stores. Plutonium is not only much rarer, it is also by far the most lethal substance in the known universe. There is not a large market for it any more because retailers who overstocked tended to get vaporized. (Large enough amounts will explode spontaneously.) However, as the former Soviet Union continues to deteriorate, the availability of weapons-grade plutonium continues to rise, so you may be able to find some on the cheap in the near future.

2: <u>Weighing your atom</u> There are two main uranium isotopes, uranium 235 and uranium 238. You will have to sort through your uranium atoms and pick out the U235. This will be very time-consuming, as U235 is exceedingly rare. It may help to use a scale: U238 weighs three more than U235, so set the tare accordingly.

Hopefully, you bought a lot of uranium. (Important note: while doing this, do not ingest any uranium, and be sure to wash your hands thoroughly.) Discard the U238 appropriately by flushing it down the toilet.

3: <u>Splitting your atom</u> Now that you've gotten a fair amount of U235, you're going to have to find a way to split it. Don't bother to try using a knife. This will not work. Not even the Ginsu knife. Instead, you are going to have to buy some neutrons. What you will need to do is propel a neutron into your U235 atom. Aim very carefully; you want to hit the middle, also known as the "nucleus." There are many different methods you can try. Some choose to grab a handful of neutrons and just hurl them at the uranium. This may work, but it is very wasteful, and neutrons don't just grow on trees. If you can find one, a neutron gun is an effective tool, but these are usually only available in some parts of the 23rd century. The two preferred techniques are A: finding a source that naturally emits neutrons, such as radium, and putting it in a glass tube with a small opening at one end or, B: using a straw—put the neutrons in your mouth and fashion a "neutron spitball", then blow through the straw toward the uranium. This is our recommended method, as it is much cheaper. (Note: do not confuse the two and put the radium in your mouth.)

4: <u>Critical mass</u> Once you have successfully split the atom, you will notice one very important thing: you didn't blow up. The problem is that you only split one atom. This produces less energy than a cat having a gastric incident. Here is where critical mass comes in. We went with uranium not just because it's bigger, but also because when it splits it gives off energy AND two neutrons. What you want to do is put all of your U235 atoms together in a big sphere, about the size of a bowling ball. (Note: this will be very heavy.) This way, when one uranium atom splits, it sends off two neutrons that hit two other atoms, which also split, giving off two neutrons, an on it goes.

This is called a "chain reaction." To extend the analogy, if one cat having a gastric incident caused two cats to have a gastric incident, and if you had one billion cats in one room together when it happened, you would have a rather impressive explosion that you would probably not want to see for yourself.

5: <u>Lead</u> You will want to seal your ball of uranium in lead. This is in case the neutrons miss, which is very possible since you aren't aiming the ones that come from the split atoms. With the lead seal, the neutrons will keep on bouncing around until they find another atom to split. Be sure to leave a small opening so you can shoot a neutron into the uranium mass to get the whole thing going.

6: <u>Don't ever try it</u> The goal of having your very own atomic bomb is letting everyone know you've got one. We recommend never actually using it, especially since you will likely not have time to get yourself a safe distance away after spitting your neutron at it, unless you have an exceptionally long straw. If people don't believe it's a real bomb, paint "atomic bomb" on the outside.

HOW TO AVOID A SPEEDING TICKET

A speeding ticket is what's known in insurance circles as a "moving violation." Insurance companies love moving violations because it gives them the opportunity to increase your premium. Likewise, many states perform interesting math in order to determine the cost of your ticket. In our state the cost is fifty dollars for the first ten miles over the limit and fifty dollars for each additional mile. Thus if you—like so many other motorists on our nation's highways—prefer to travel at Warp Factor Nine, you may have to mortgage your home to cover the cost of the ticket and the increase in your premium.

1: <u>Don't speed</u> This is commonsense advice that may be more difficult than it at first appears due to a variety of factors. Below are some very valid causes of speeding:

—Your wife is in labor
—You are in labor
—You are listening to Led Zeppelin II
—You have a powerful need to catch up with that asshole that cut you off five miles ago so that you can choke the miserable life from his worthless body
—You live in Massachusetts
—A robot from the future is chasing you

—The timer on the bomb in your trunk can't be reset and you're not at the target yet

2: <u>Don't get caught</u> If you must speed—if, for instance, you and your wife are in labor while driving through Massachusetts fleeing a robot from the future who is trying to get to the bomb in your trunk before you catch up to the guy who cut you off right in the middle of "Heartbreaker"—you should do everything you can to not get caught. It helps to know the warning signs indicating a police presence, such as:

—The guy ahead of you suddenly slowing down and changing lanes
—Oncoming traffic blinking their headlights at you as they pass
—Any sign that reads "State Police Next Exit"
—Blue flashing lights
—Stray gunfire

3: <u>Talk your way out of it</u> Under certain circumstances, it is possible to talk your way out of a speeding ticket. Here are some dos and don'ts.

DO act exceedingly polite. If you have had little practice in being polite, it essentially involves adding as many words as possible to your sentences. For example, saying "What's the problem, bud?" is far less polite than "Whatever is the matter, my dear sir?"

DO be English, or at least have a good fake accent. We once met a cab driver who talked his way out of a speeding ticket by claiming he thought the highway number was the speed limit. He was on Route 95 at the time. Try this.

DO NOT be black. Even if you're not speeding, it is in your best interest to not be black if you do not wish to be pulled over.

DO NOT offer any bribes if the largest bill you have on you is a twenty. You'll just look silly.

DO be an attractive female. Not only will this improve your chances of getting out of a speeding ticket, it offers a nice view for the rest of us when we drive by.

DO NOT have a live person in the trunk. They'll start kicking and shouting, which will make it much harder for you to convince the officer that you're just an honest citizen covered in your own blood.

DO NOT get out of your car to plead your case. They will shoot you on principle.

4: <u>Run for it</u> As we have all learned from watching classics such as "Dukes of Hazard" and "Smokey and the Bandit," when you flee the police they will gang up on you until there are so many cruisers giving chase they start to run into each other, resulting in comical fifteen car pileups where nobody actually gets hurt. Please remember to go "Yeeehaaaah!" at least once.

PART II

※

ON NOT GETTING EATEN OR OTHERWISE PERMANENTLY DAMAGED

—How to Survive a Shark Attack

—How to Fend Off an Attack From an Extradimensional Invader From the Planet Nebulon Four

—How to Fend Off a Squirrel

—How to Get Away From a Bear

—How to Tell When Your Dog is Rabid

—How to Deal With Foreigners

—How to Avoid Alien Abduction

—How to Survive a Bad Movie

—How to Deal With a Cat Infestation

HOW TO SURVIVE A SHARK ATTACK

1: <u>Don't swim in the ocean</u> Ninety-nine percent of all shark attacks take place in exceptionally large bodies of water also known as oceans. The way to determine if you are currently in an ocean is to taste the water, which should be salty. (Exception: the Dead Sea.)

2: <u>Listen for the music</u> In the event that you are foolish enough to recreate in an ocean, listen carefully for the music, as demonstrated in the marvelous documentary film *JAWS*. All shark attacks are preceded by the "daah-da, daah-da" chords, which will gradually become more rapid as the shark gets closer. This is due to the doppler effect.

3: <u>Swim with fat people</u> Try to surround yourself with more appetizing companions. If you know them well, you might even try to switch their suntan lotion with A-1 Steak Sauce. This will definitely improve your odds.

4: <u>Don't panic</u> In the event that a shark actually bites you, try to remain calm. This really won't help you survive, but everyone else on the beach will appreciate you not shrieking madly, as this is quite unsettling.

Kinds of Shark Attacks

—<u>The "hello" bite</u> Sharks are not equipped with the appropriate vocal devices to hold a proper conversation. Often, they are just curious about the weather. Always watch the latest weather report prior to entering the ocean, and be ready to shout this information to the shark. They may still bite you, but it would only be a "thanks" bite, which is not nearly as dangerous.

—<u>The bump and run</u> Often, the shark just needs a dance partner. They are very proud, such that even though all sharks are uniformly poor dancers, each one thinks he or she is quite good at it and will refuse to dance with other sharks. The shark probably thinks you are a seal (seals are very good dancers.) So if the shark bumps up into you a couple of times, do your best seal impression. If he is sober, he will swim away in a few minutes. If drunk, the shark will dance for quite some time, and then attempt to mate with you.

—<u>The cinematic bite</u> Easily the most dangerous type of shark attack, this only takes place in the presence of movie cameras. The shark will either pull you dramatically under the water, letting you go long enough to scream and then pulling you under again, or, he will come up out of the water and eat you whole. On film, it's remarkably dramatic. Unfortunately, it is also somewhat lethal.

HOW TO FEND OFF AN ATTACK FROM AN EXTRADIMENSIONAL INVADER FROM THE PLANET NEBULON FOUR

The beings from the planet Nebulon Four are very aggressive in nature and have developed a taste for the human Medulla Oblongata (which is somewhere in the brain, we think.) They are not to be confused with the docile "pod people" of Nebulon Five. Before taking agressive action of any kind, count the tentacles. Invaders from Nebulon Four have six tentacles, whereas Nebulon Five inhabitants have eight.

1: <u>Go ahead and panic</u> This will buy you some time, as the Nebulon Four invaders are unfamiliar with human emotions. Running around, screaming, calling out to your mother, wetting yourself, etc., will confuse them.

2: <u>Stay out of their grasp for as long as possible</u> You will not be able to outrun them, because they can run very quickly due to having grown up on a large planet with a greater gravitational pull. They will often fall for the "what's that over there?" trick, especially since they have only one eye.

3: <u>Avoid the mouth</u> Do not assume that the small opening below their noses is the mouth; it is not. That orifice is used exclusively for smoking Parliaments. The mouth is underneath their torso in the middle of their six tentacles.

4: <u>Find the weak spot</u> The weak spot on invaders from Nebulon Four is between the third and fourth tentacle (counting clockwise, starting from the front left tentacle.) It is only about the size of a quarter. Punch this spot as hard as you can until it says something that sounds like "blurk." (Roughly translated, this means "oww, goddamnit!")

5: <u>Run</u> Nebulon Four invaders have a very low pain threshhold, and it will take them several minutes to recover after being hit in the weak spot. If you are nowhere in sight by the time they feel like moving again, they will look for another victim.

Things to know

Invaders from Nebulon Four are usually attracted to mad scientists and buxom blonde women. Be sure to stay away from mad scientists at all times.

HOW TO FEND OFF A SQUIRREL

1: <u>Don't panic</u> Squirrels can be very intimidating, but remember; they are probably just as scared as you.

2: <u>Don't feed it</u> Being confronted by one squirrel is daunting enough. If you have bread crumbs or nuts with you, do not offer them to the squirrel in the hopes that you can sneak away while he's eating, because what you will do instead is attract more squirrels.

3: <u>Square your shoulders</u> Face the squirrel directly and adopt the following pose: legs spread aparts and straight, hands on hips, staring straight ahead, looking vaguely bullet-proof. This pose is universally understood by squirrels to mean "I am Superman in disguise, and I am not afraid of some damn little rodent." (This pose works just as well for women, as squirrels can't tell the difference.)

4: <u>Laugh heartily</u> If the Superman pose doesn't work, try a devil-may-care laugh. This should stun the squirrel into freezing, at least momentarily.

5: <u>Do not turn your back on it</u> Most squirrels think they can take on Superman if they get a good shot at him when he's not expecting it. If you turn away, he might go for you.

6: <u>Punt</u> While the squirrel is stunned by your raucous laugh, step forward quickly and kick the squirrel as hard as you can. Bonus points if you clear the trees.

Things to know

—Many people unwisely follow the incorrect advice when confronted by a squirrel: they play dead. Squirrels do not fall for this. They will go for your eyes.

—Punted squirrels occasionally land on top of other people. While this is rare, you could be in serious trouble if one lands on you. Bring an umbrella when you stroll in the park, just in case.

HOW TO GET AWAY FROM A BEAR

1: <u>Don't go camping</u> Bears generally live in wooded areas or on ice floes. There are very few urban bears left, so you are very unlikely to come across one in the city. Even the bad parts of the city. Camping in general seems like a rather unhealthy activity, as one has to abandon oneself in the woods with little more than a canvas tent to protect oneself from rampant examples of nature in abundance in wooded regions. And don't even get us started on the mosquitos. So anyway, don't go camping.

2: <u>You went camping, didn't you?</u> Fool.

3: <u>Stay as far away from food as possible</u> This may be difficult if you want to live through your camping experience, but it wasn't our idea to go camping, now, was it? Despite being a gigantic, chubby bundle of cuteness, one bear can take on the entire Russian weightlifting team with one hand, even with the performance-enhancing drugs factored in. This bear wants your food. If you personally smell like food, you're in even worse shape. (The chef is always the first one to go, especially if he is played by a member of a minority.)

4: <u>When confronted, leave it the hell alone</u> Do not attempt to pet the bear.

5: <u>The honey trick</u> If leaving it alone isn't working, point over the bear's shoulder (either one) and say "look! Honey!" As is well documented in such classic pieces of literature as Winnie the Pooh, bears cannot resist honey. When the bear stops to look over his or her shoulder, run away.

6: <u>Appear bigger</u> Take your child, or the shortest member of your party, and put them on your shoulder. This says to the bear one of two things: "I am a very large human with extra arms" or "here, take the child. Just don't hurt me." In either case, you should be safe.

7: <u>Take a hostage</u> If none of the above has worked, get a hold of a bear cub. Say something along the lines of "one more move and the cub gets it!" Then back away until you reach the car—which is hopefully nearby—and drive away fast. Keep the cub if you want.

HOW TO TELL WHEN YOUR DOG IS RABID

1: <u>She won't come when called</u> This is assuming that at one time the dog did come when called. This by itself is not a sure sign that the dog is rabid, so don't jump to conclusions. She could just be trapped under something heavy.

2: <u>Persistent growling, at everything, including fleas</u>

3: <u>She starts to answer to the name "Cujo"</u> It may be a good idea to try this name out once a week or so, just to be sure. If she starts responding, look out.

4: <u>Inability to walk a straight line</u> This also may be an indication that she has a drinking problem. Check for alcohol on the breath.

5: <u>Foaming at the mouth</u> There is also the outside possibility she has simply eaten a bar of soap. Taste the foam to be sure.

6: <u>She kills a guy</u> This is a bad sign. However, before taking steps to deal with your dog, consider that you might be held culpable. Be sure to bury the body someplace, before anyone notices.

7: <u>Other behavioral changes</u> If your dog already does not come when called, foams at the mouth on occasion, drinks in excess, growls every day, kills a guy every now and then, and is named Cujo, you may have to rely on other signs. Rabies affects the dog's mental processes, so be on the lookout for indications of mental deteriorization. For instance, if instead of chasing her tail she chases the neighborhood children, you should note this. She will start to lose her memory as well. For example, she may forget what her dog food looks like, and attempt to eat you instead. Also, many rabid dogs develop a strong urge to cross-dress. Be wary.

What to do

Once you are certain your dog is rabid, you should probably shoot her immediately. Bury her next to the guy she killed.

HOW TO DEAL WITH FOREIGNERS

Unfortunately, many foreign countries are overrun with foreigners, most of whom do not even speak English. You run a serious risk of encountering one if you leave the country. Foreigners have also been known to migrate to areas within the United States. Be wary.

1: <u>Don't panic</u> They are probably just as scared of you as you are of them. Sudden movements may provoke them.

2: <u>Find out what they want</u> Communication with a foreigner can be very difficult, especially when they do not speak English. Attempt non-verbal communication.

3: <u>Speak loudly</u> If non-verbal communcation fails, try speaking to them. English, when spoken in a normal tone, can only be understood by persons who are fluent in it. But when spoken loudly or shouted, by saying for instance "WHAT DO YOU WANT" as if you were speaking to a person hard of hearing, it can be comprehended by all.

4: <u>Standard questions</u> Here are five common questions to try. Memorize them. 1) Do you need directions? 2) Do you have a bomb or weapon of some kind? 3) Are you the waiter? 4) Is this your cab? 5) Was that your ox I just hit?

5: <u>Offer them money</u> If you are still unable to find out what the foreign person needs so that they might go away, give them some money.

Things to know

Amazingly, in many foreign cultures, Americans are considered foreigners.

HOW TO AVOID ALIEN ABDUCTION

1: <u>Reside in or near a city</u> Aliens are partial to remote, isolated regions, so much so that if given the choice between abducting someone a second or third time from a farm or nabbing someone new who lives in a metropolitan area, they will pick the former.

2: <u>Have an uninteresting ass</u> This is an admittedly nebulous directive, since nobody is really sure what the aliens are looking for. (Some have suggested that they lost their keys in someone years ago and are still trying to find them.) However, an anal probe should figure prominently in their examination. You might even consider getting a small tattoo on your lower back that reads "nothing to see here." Others have taped themselves shut each night with duct tape. This does not work, and is also quite painful.

3: <u>Be skeptical</u> In the history of alien abduction, no vocally skeptical person has ever been taken. *a priori* belief just makes you more attractive to them.

4: <u>Don't sleep in your bed</u> If you do happen to reside in a rural area, construct a dummy of yourself and put it in your bed every night. You should sleep in the basement. Important: be sure to include an anus on your dummy. That's what they'll be looking for.

5: <u>Do not allow yourself to be hypnotized</u> Given enough time, a hypnotist will discover that you have been abducted, even if you personally don't think this is the case. The best way to avoid this problem is to just not get hypnotized at all.

If you have been abducted

There are many national organizations that will want to hear your story, such as: the National Inquirer, the Weekly World News, and the Mutual UFO Network (MUFON.) You may want to secure the services of an agent before negotiating, especially if you've had a particularly interesting abduction experience. Do not accept anything under six figures.

HOW TO SURVIVE A BAD MOVIE

It has been well-documented that the viewing a genuinely bad movie can result in a number of adverse effects, such as: blindness, insanity, madness, extreme stupidity, vacuousness, and People Magazine subscriptions.

Much like pregnancy, the best way to avoid a bad movie is to abstain. Consequently, we will concentrate initially on learning to recognize a bad movie in advance.

<u>Stars</u> Who is starring in the film? Did they also produce and/or write the film? This is a warning sign, known hereafter as the "Hudson Hawk" rule.

Be especially aware of the following actors.

—Kevin Costner. Not only will this in all likelihood be an extremely bad film, it will probably also last at least four hours. Case in point: *Wyatt Earp* which lasted as long as Mr. Earp's actual life.

—Robin Williams. We are not sure when Mr. Williams transformed from edgy comic to freakishly unfunny "family film" actor, but we think it might have been around the time he stopped using cocaine. Exception: he's usually okay in minor or supporting roles. This is known as the Whoopi Goldberg rule.

—Eddie Murphy. A very gifted comic actor who unfortunately looks in the mirror and sees Jerry Lewis. And Lewis did it better, which speaks volumes. The Whoopi Goldberg rule also applies here. Example: *Bowfinger*.

—John Travolta. Yes, Mr. Travolta has acted in a few very good films, i.e., *Pulp Fiction*. However, if you avoid his larger body of work altogether, the percentages will definitely be in your favor. He is also a Scientologist, which means he's more than a little crazy. This is also known as the Tom Cruise rule.

—Leonardo DiCaprio. We were probably the only person watching *Titanic* who cheered when DiCaprio's character finally died. We expect him to join the Church of Scientology any day now. Our advice is to see *What's Eating Gilbert Grape* and then never see another film with DiCaprio in it.

Reviews Reading reviews can be very instructive, but what you really want to look for are films that are not reviewed at all. If, on the day the film opens, you see a note in the paper stating that the "film was not made available for review" do NOT see the film under any circumstances. This means the movie is so bad even the studio doesn't want you to see it.

Musicals Almost without exception, a musical made later than 1975 is a bad movie. In some cases they are not just bad, they are spectacularly bad. We rented *Moulin Rouge* and discovered that it was easily the worst film ever made. Never before has a movie showed such base disrespect for the songs they were ransacking. For example, Ewan MacGregor sang Elton John's "Your Song" with a heavy orchestral background, an angelic choir, and the weakest damn voice you've ever heard. At one point he sang to Nicole Kidman that he'd forgotten if her eyes were green or blue WHILE LOOKING INTO HER EYES. This movie actually had the temerity to play Nirvana's "Smells Like Teen Spirit" as a DANCE NUMBER. Anyway, it was a bad movie, and we hated it, so don't see it. Exception to 1975 rule: *Hedwig and the Angry Inch.*

Demographics Sometimes a film may be considered bad simply because you are not a member of the target demographic. Please review the following categories.

—Teen Movies. This is any movie that takes place in a school; involves girls who are supposed to be ugly according to the script but are actually just wearing glasses; stars Freddy Prinze Jr., a pop singer, the Wayans Brothers, or any cast member of Dawson's Creek; or has a killer running around who is offing people in ludicrous ways for totally random and absurd reasons. These films are targeted toward teenagers and pedophiles.

—Porn Films. In a porn film, graphic sex takes place every ten minutes, using positions that are physiologically impossible involving men who evidently have penises in their navels and women who apparently have one or two extra orifices. Plot and acting is virtually non-existent because most of the budget was spent on camcorders and breast implants. By definition, the porn film is a bad film. However, the targeted demographic is heterosexual males, and their judgment is often skewed when there is a naked woman on the screen.

—Chick Flicks. There are a number of ways to define the chick flick; the scope of the definition widens in direct proportion to the testosterone levels of the definer. For example, we know many males who identify any film wherein "nobody's blowing up shit" as a chick flick. We will narrow the parameters slightly, as follows: any love story; any film starring Meg Ryan or Emma Thompson; any period piece starring Ralph Fiennes; any Merchant-Ivory production. A classic example of a chick flick: *The English Patient*, which is a love story starring Ralph Fiennes and made by Merchant-Ivory. Not only is this a chick flick, it is long enough to qualify as a Kevin Costner film.

<u>Good Bad Movies</u> Sometimes, Hollywood makes a bad film on purpose. This can make matters difficult for the moviegoer, insofar as it may be difficult to ascertain whether a movie is genuinely bad or entertainingly bad. The easiest way to tell the difference is to study the actors to determine whether or not they are taking themselves seriously within the context of their performance. For example, Sylvester Stallone always takes himself very seriously, and has absolutely no comic timing whatsoever. Consequently, when he says a line that is meant to be funny, it is not, and when he says a serious line, it is often delivered so poorly it ends up being funny. Conversely, Kevin Bacon and Fred Ward in *Tremors* know fully well that they are in a movie that is intentionally bad, and therefore end up turning in serious performances that are also funny. This is also known as "kitsch." (There are rare occasions when a film is so bad that despite the efforts of the filmmakers to take themselves seriously it still ends up developing a cult following, which automatically classifies it as kitsch. Example: *Showgirls*.)

<u>Surviving a Bad Movie</u>

If you have missed the warning signs for a bad movie you may find yourself in one of two situations: trapped in a dark movie theater with strangers, or in your living room watching it on tape or DVD. We offer solutions for both.

<u>Movie Theater</u>

1: <u>Do not panic</u> When being confronted by a mind-bogglingly awful film panic can be very dangerous, as panic is often followed by disorientation, nausea, and loud shrieking.

2: <u>Do not comment</u> Your instinctive reaction will be to let everyone else in the theater know exactly how bad you think the movie is. What you are saying is "I'm not the sort of idiot who thinks this movie is good." The problem is, you may be sitting near a person who is actually enjoying the film, and may take offense. You may even be married to them—as was the case when we saw *Dungeons and Dragons*.

3: <u>Locate the exits</u> The exits should be clearly marked at the front and back of the theater, and have been cleared of any potential obstructions. The theater owners go through the trouble of telling you this in advance. They say it's "in case of fire" but the real reason is that back in the late Sixties, hundreds of people attempted to flee the theater while the horrifically bad film *Blow Up* was being aired, and many lawsuits ensued.

4: <u>Calmly exit the theater</u> Do not look back. Remember Lot's wife.

5: <u>Get your money back</u> You may try to get your money back from the theater if you leave early enough. What you should do is ask for the manager, who may give you passes for a future bad film. There is the possibility that the manager will not give you anything, figuring it was your own fault for electing to witness a bad movie in the first place. If this happens, pretend you are having a heart attack, and have the person you're with negotiate for passes while the ambulance takes you away.

<u>At Home</u>

1: <u>Turn off the VCR or DVD</u> As soon as you realize the film you have rented is irredeemably bad, shut it off and get it out of your VCR or DVD player immediately.

2: <u>Disinfect</u> Your VCR or DVD player may have picked up bad movie germs, which will corrupt future films. For the next six months, you will find yourself thinking "hey, this reminds me of that really crappy movie" no matter what movie you're actually watching at the time. To disinfect, replace the bad film with *The Godfather Part Two*, a movie all households should be equipped with at all times. Note: if your DVD player is in your personal computer, you may also need to run anti-virus software.

3: <u>Destroy the film</u> Returning the movie to the rental store is as irresponsible as leaving a loaded gun on the sidewalk. Most rental stores recognize the public service you will be providing by rendering the film unwatchable for future unsuspecting households. Return the empty box with a note explaining the actions you have taken and the reason. You may find a nice credit or two has been added to your account the next time you rent a movie. When we did this with the movie *Very Bad Things*, we actually received applause from the rental store employees.

<u>Things To Know</u>

—The U.S. Army has used the animated feature film *Happily Ever After* as a means to elicit confessions from terrorism suspects, with great success.

—Cable television is where bad movies go to die. Be extremely careful when flipping through the channels, and especially avoid films that are sequels to movies you never heard of in the first place. This is a major warning sign.

—Steven Segal films are one of the leading causes of madness in this country today.

HOW TO DEAL WITH A CAT INFESTATION

The house cat, much like the common house fly, is an unwelcome pest in any home. Unfortunately, whereas eliminating flies involves little more than a can of Raid and a little free time, cats are much more difficult to catch, kill, and dispose of.

1: <u>Identify the problem</u> The most important initial step is to identify whether or not you do in fact have a cat problem. For instance, you may actually have a rat, a mouse, or a small dog. The common signs of a cat infestation include:

—loud scurrying about the house at three in the morning
—the smell of pee in various parts of the house, including your sock drawer
—random keys pressed on your keyboard when you've left the room
—broken shards of what used to be an expensive family heirloom scattered across your living room floor
—something with a furry tail brushing against your feet and then disappearing suddenly (non-furry tail means it is a rat)
—tell-tale scratches on your extremities
—waking up in the middle of the night feeling like there is a large weight on your chest

2: <u>Test for poltergeists</u> There is an outside chance that you actually have a poltergeist in your home and not a cat. Just to be safe, call a priest and have him bless the house (keep him away from the children) and then see if the above problems continue.

3: <u>Set traps</u> Cats are very smart, and they hide very well, especially if you are looking for them. Rather than actively hunt them, your best bet may be to set up passive lures. One such lure is a "cat box." This is a plastic box filled with "kitty litter" that you may set up in any room of the house. Cats will come out to use the bathroom in this box, especially if you've remembered to shut your sock drawer. You may have to hide and wait for the cat to come out and then pounce on them, as cat boxes are not designed to ensnare cats for some reason. Another option is to put out "cat food." Do not attempt to poison the cat food, as we have tried this and it does not work.

4: <u>Catnip</u> If the food and the cat box do not work, try to obtain a small quantity of "catnip." This is a federally controlled substance, but may be obtained at a reasonable price in Mexico. Take the catnip, and load it into a water bong. Leave the bong and a lighter in the middle of the room. No cat can resist.

5: <u>Extermination</u> Once you have lured the cat into the open, you will have to exterminate it. There is unfortunately no "Raid for cats" on the market right now, so you may have to rely on small arms. We recommend a .22 caliber handgun. Anything larger will create a terrible mess. If you do not have access to a gun, you may be forced to grab the still-living feline. Be very careful; cats have sharp claws, and they bite. There is no telling what sort of diseases they are carrying around. Once you've grabbed the cat try to stun it by hitting it against a heavy object such as a desk or table.

6: <u>Disposal</u> If you are dealing with a non-dead cat, you are going to have to dispose of it in a way that ensures it will never return. (Cats are vindictive.) Swinging it by the tail and then hurling it as far as you can, while a great deal of fun, may not do the trick. One popular method is to put the cat in a sack and throw it into a river. If you are not near a river or have no sack, simply place the unconscious pest into a cardboard box, tape the box shut, and leave the box on the median strip of a major highway late at night. Do not try to flush the cat down the toilet, as we have tried this, and it does not work.

Things to know

—As odd as it may seem, in many parts of the world people actually keep cats as pets!

—Eating a cat may seem like a viable disposal option, but we do not recommend it, as there is very little meat on them, and they taste rather gamey.

—Scientists recently cloned a cat, which proves beyond a doubt that scientists can be pretty damned weird.

PART III

SUICIDAL TENDENCIES

—How to Jump to Your Death

—How to Drink and Drive

—How to Start a Militia

—How to Conjure Up a Demon

—How to Reach the Summit of Mt. Everest

—How to Tell if Your Husband Is In the Mafia

—How to Streak During a Major League Baseball Game

—How to Cross a Busy Street

HOW TO JUMP TO YOUR DEATH

1: <u>Select a building, bridge or other location of great height</u> It is important to choose a site where, should one plummet from the top, sufficient descending speed is attained. Minimum height should be no less than three hundred feet. For the inventive suicide, consider going skydiving without a parachute.

2: <u>Avoid ledges</u> Standing on a ledge and "thinking it over" will only prolong the process, because then the police will send someone out to try to talk you out of it. This will only confuse matters.

3: <u>Gain separation</u> If you are jumping from a solid vertical structure—such as a building—you will have to push yourself away from the structure far enough to avoid striking the side of the structure on the way down. This may require some practice. Try to avoid buildings with balconies, awnings, and flagpoles. There is nothing more embarrassing than attempting suicide and ending up with only a broken leg.

4: <u>Curl into a ball</u> While descending, your worst enemy is wind shear. Curl into a ball and hug your knees to cut down on resistance.

5: <u>Avoid superheroes</u> Many superheroes will try to save you. Try to jump at a time when they are busy fighting an evil menace on the other end of town.

HOW TO DRINK AND DRIVE

Drinking and driving is of course not in any way recommended. In the last two years alone, drinking and driving caused more legislation in the United States than any other unrecommended act, including bungee jumping.

1: <u>Start drinking</u> There wouldn't be much point to a section called "How To Drink And Drive" if drinking wasn't included in the instructions. If you intend to drive later, make an earnest effort to drink in moderation. If you have difficulty determining if you have been drinking in moderation, check for these symptoms of excessive alcohol consumption:

A) You are uncertain as to the current location of your pants.

B) You know where your pants are, but they are on your head instead of where they should be.

C) You're having trouble understanding symptom B (above) because you believe you are supposed to be wearing your pants on your head.

D) The band stopped playing an hour ago but you are still talking very loudly.

E) You have no idea what the drink in your hand is called, or even how it got into your hand in the first place. Or if it's even your drink.

F) The word "dude" has become very important to you.

G)You've hit on everyone in the room and are now trying to take home a potted plant.

H) The bartender shut you off an hour ago, so now you're bribing people to get drinks for you and stealing unattended ones.

I) You get physically ill, and enjoy the experience.

J) Someone puts out a cigarette in your drink and you drink it anyway.

2: <u>Locate your keys</u> Hopefully, for all our sakes, somebody has already taken them from you. If this has not happened, you should find them in your pants, which are on your head.

3: <u>Locate your car</u> This should be approximately where you left it. Try to remember where that is.

4: <u>Start driving</u> If you cannot recall how to drive, don't try. Just lie down in the front seat and sleep it off.

5: <u>Find the median</u> That would be the dotted or solid line down the middle of the street. The correct position for your car is to the RIGHT of this line. Do not drive to the left of it unless you are in England. (We do not recommend drinking and driving in England.) Follow the median carefully. Not only does this keep you from running into the cars coming from the opposite direction, but it is the universally recognized symbol of outright drunkenness. Your fellow drivers will appreciate your forthrightness and will know to avoid you. The police might even pull you over to congratulate you for doing this right.

6: <u>Find your way home</u> There is only so much detail a book of this sort can go into. Unfortunately, we do not know where you live. If you are equally uncertain, you might wish to consider stopping and asking others "Do you know where I live?" There is a decent chance that your license has your current address, so you may also want to check that. The police can also be very helpful on this matter.

HOW TO START A MILITIA

1: <u>Hate the government</u> The very first step in starting your own militia is to learn to hate the government intensely. This should not be all that hard.

2: <u>Become very paranoid</u> Okay, everybody hates the government. But once you've exhausted your list of perfectly legitimate reasons to hate the government, you're going to have to expand a bit. Most professional militia-starters jump straight on to their "why my life sucks in general" list. You are going to have to first make this list, and then come up with reasons why the items on this list are also the government's fault. You will have to get very creative, and probably ascribe abilities to the government that are not only wholly beyond both the capability of any modern governing apparatus, but are also beyond the capabilty of modern technology.

> Example: "Bobby-Sue broke up with me in seventh grade." Whose fault? "The government." How? "Using alien tracking technology that was reverse-engineered from the Roswell UFO, they compelled Bobby-Sue to think I was dumb and smelled funny, and they even made her say I kiss like a sick trout." Why would they do this? "To crush my spirit and keep me down so I would offer less resistance when they come for me."

Now that you see how it's done, get to work.

3: <u>Move to Montana</u> This is where all the best militias go, although other Midwest states will also work very well.

4: <u>Get guns</u> You are going to need a tremendous amount of guns. Fortunately, thanks to the tireless efforts of the National Rifle Association, it is now possible to buy in bulk.

5: <u>Develop a manifesto</u> You are now highly paranoid, isolated, and heavily armed, which means you're almost there. Now is the time to develop a manifesto that establishes your beliefs as to how the government should run things and what you plan to do about it. Literacy and reason need not go anywhere near your manifesto. It does, however, need to clearly identify your desire to overthrow the current government with violence. This will become critical during the recruitment period.

> Example: Do NOT say: "We will take over the government by presenting the American people with a viable third-party candidate." DO say: "We will bathe in the blood of the oppressor, destroy their false idols, and T.P. the White House."

If, at this point, it is occurring to you that there is no earthly way a small band of heavily armed but thoroughly disorganized nutjobs could possibly overthrow the entire United States government, you are far too intelligent to start a militia. Sell the guns and get out of Montana, before it's too late.

6: <u>Recruit</u> This is the easy part. There are several online resources available to you for recruiting, and if you're too paranoid to trust the internet, well, you're in Montana. Just walk around and talk to people. Follow the checklist, below, to identify potential recruits. (Seven out of ten equals a good recruiting prospect.)

If he:

—Has not bathed recently

—Is very well armed

—Thinks you might be a government agent

—Is wearing aluminum foil on his head to prevent the government from "reading thoughts"

—Cannot read your manifesto because it has too many big words

—Drives a pickup truck with a passenger side door held closed with a bent coat hanger

—Hasn't had a full set of teeth for twenty years

—Thinks the NRA is too liberal

—Takes pride in being home-schooled

—Thinks that being politically correct means using the word "coon" instead of "nigger"

7: <u>Piss off the government</u> This might seem illogical, because getting the attention of the same government you intend to overthrow now, before you have adequate numbers to do so, seems rather stupid. Here is the reasoning you need to master for this step to make sense.

A: the government already knows all about me

B: they consider me a huge threat, because I'm such a damned important person

C: they will be coming for me soon

D: if I give them an excuse to come after me, I'll be less likely to be surprised

E: this will confirm my opinion of myself as a damned important person, and not a total loser

So, after establishing an organization (at least five people) it is time for you to secede from the union. Specifically, this means that you declare that you no longer intend to pay taxes. If this does not get the government's attention (for instance, if you never had a large enough income to declare in the first place) you might want to consider printing your own money. If this fails as well, try blowing something up. Eventually, your compound will be surrounded by heavily armed government employees. Congratulations!

HOW TO CONJURE UP A DEMON

There are as many different ways to conjure up a demon as there are demons to conjure. What we offer is a basic, step-by-step approach that should work in most cases, but please note that additional precautions will be necessary when attempting to conjure any members of the Unholy Echelon of the Seventh Ring of Drakul. The Sixth and Eighth Rings, however, are fine. Also, in the event that you manage to conjure Lord Chthulu, please contact the authors, as he owes us ten bucks.

You will need:

—Kosher salt
—The right testicle of a Scandinavian (male) toad*
—A recently deceased feline
—The blood of a virgin, type AB negative*
—A heavy cloak
—a book of matches
—a scrap of paper autographed by Margaret Thatcher (substitutions allowed: Madonna, Uther Pendragon, or the shy member of N'SYNC)
—A tuna sandwich, on rye

*Available in specialty shops

1: <u>Isolate yourself</u> You will need to find an unoccupied enclosed space, such as a basement or an abandoned warehouse. Wooded areas are not recommended, because they're kinda spooky.

2: <u>Wait until Midnight</u> Many explanations have been given for this, and most of them are unnecessarily mystical in nature. The truth is, it's easier to catch a demon when they're asleep. While you're waiting for Midnight, take off all your clothes and put on the heavy cloak. This is in order to avoid getting tell-tale stains on your clothing.

3: <u>Inscribe a pentangle</u> Take the kosher salt and use it to make a pentangle on the floor. (A pentangle is a five-cornered star.) Do not use regular salt. This is important, but we have no idea why. Once you have finished the pentangle, stand in the center and face the bottom, i.e., not one of the points. Face the wrong direction and you will be performing "white" magic rather than "black" magic, and before you know it you've conjured an angel by accident. This can be very embarrassing, and could get you into a great deal of trouble. Plus, angels are rather dull.

4: <u>A circle and a cat</u> This can get icky. Make a circle in the center of the pentangle with the virgin blood. From this point on you should not step outside the circle, and you should definitely not step out of the pentangle. (If you must know why, the virgin blood is to attract the demon—they're partial toward virgins—and the salt is to keep them from touching you, as demons are members of the slug genus.) Now, gut the cat. You will discover that the cat is full of a bunch of goop. Remove the goop slowly while reciting the name of the demon you wish to conjure and flinging cat parts toward each point of the star. Do this until you run out of goop. This will wake the demon up and draw his or her attention because frankly, throwing cat guts around is a damned strange thing to do.

5: <u>Final steps</u> Now that the nastiest part is out of the way, eat the tuna sandwich, because you might have a long wait and we wouldn't want you to do that on an empty stomach. Finally, once your demon has made his or her appearance, command the demon to do whatever it is you want them to do, and then light the scrap of paper using the matches to seal the "contract."

Things to know

—Occasionally, people conjuring demons have inadvertently been possessed by them. In the event that you become possessed, do not panic. What you need to do is find an outlet for the demon to indulge his or her evil tendencies. This can result in killing sprees, which are bad. To sate your demon, join the Republican party immediately.

—It is a good idea to already know what you want your demon to do before starting, as they can be extremely impatient. Also, they are not that bright, so make it something simple, like "kill Detroit" rather than "solve Fermat's last theorem."

—Demons are loud, large, ugly, uncommonly smelly, and generally the most frightening thing you've ever seen in your entire life. You will very much want to run away. Don't. Your demon is more than a little bit pissed off right now, especially since you've woken him up, and the salt is the only thing stopping him from doing very bad things to you, things that will make you think the cat got off easy. Don't say we didn't warn you.

HOW TO REACH THE SUMMIT OF MOUNT EVEREST

At 29,028 feet above sea level, the top of Mount Everest is the highest point on Earth. It is a very stupid place to be. Please take our word for it and don't go. Seriously, it's a bad idea. If you want to get high above sea level, take an airplane. They cruise at that altitude.

Okay, fine. Be that way.

There is very little in the way of practical instruction that we can give you other than "keep climbing until you run out of things to climb." This would make for a very short chapter. What we have tried to do instead is offer a little advice and give you an idea of what to expect as you ascend.

To summit Mount Everest, you will need:

—Warm clothing
—Boots that you've already worn a few times
—Icepick
—Backpack
—U.V.-blocking goggles
—Crampons (these are not feminine products; they are metal spikes that clip onto boots)

—A death wish
—Bottled oxygen
—Excess body fat you don't mind getting rid of
—Food

1: <u>Go to Nepal</u> Nepal is a country somewhere near the bottom of Mount Everest, although we are not altogether sure where as we do not have an atlas with us right now. It is also possible to summit Mount Everest from China, but you will need to get permission from China first, and this is difficult, because China doesn't like you. Do not anger China.

2: <u>Hire sherpas</u> The only thing dumber than trying to reach the top of Mount Everest is doing is alone. In Nepalese, the word "sherpa" translates as "foolish, and probably insane." You can understand, then, why it would be good to have a few around. Sherpas will help guide you up the mountain, can carry your equipment for you, and make excellent witnesses at the inquest.

3: <u>Locate Mount Everest</u> This should be the tallest mountain there. You are welcome to scale some of the other mountains instead, but this could create a problem in the future when you attempt to brag, as many of these mountains have very odd names. "I summited Ama Dablam" not only means nothing to most people, it sounds as if you are perhaps recounting a sexual exploit.

4: <u>Climb to Everest Base Camp</u> Fortuitously, Everest has a number of rest stops that will be very helpful to you. These are natural flat areas that have been built up over time due to the large amount of traffic heading up and down the mountain. Base camp is only at about seventeen thousand feet, and should be no problem for you. Eat at the Denny's and stay a while.

5: <u>Camp One</u> To reach this camp, you're going to have to navigate an area called "icefall," so named because it's full of ice that may just fall.

This is absurdly dangerous because the ice we are talking about is enormous blocks called "seracs," and when they fall, they will kill you in a very permanent way. Provided you survive the icefall, you will find camp one very pleasant, although you will be unable to enjoy much of it because you will be too busy gasping desperately for breath. You are almost at twenty thousand feet right now, and oxygen—which is much smarter than you—doesn't really hang out at this altitude that often. Spend a few days at camp one to get used to the thin air.

6: <u>Camp Two</u> As you ascend to the second camp—over 21,000 feet—you will begin to notice certain "hints" that perhaps man was not meant to occupy this particular region of our planet (Earth.) One hint is that you have to wear a heavily tinted sun visor at all times because you will otherwise be permanently blinded by UV radiation that's usually blocked by the ozone layer you're currently standing in. Another hint is that there is only 50% of the recommended daily allowance of oxygen at this height. Also, it's about thirty degrees below zero with the wind. And if none of that registers, take a look at all the dead people lying in the snow drifts along the path.

7: <u>Camp Three</u> Now that you have reached the 24,000 foot mark, it is time to reacquiant yourself with the signs of frostbite. Look for red patches of skin that have no feeling to them. Roughly sixty percent of your body should feel this way. On the plus side, you're losing brain cells by the thousand, so there is a good chance you don't even care about the frostbite. You will find a larger supply of extra human corpses at this height, and you might even spot a Yeti if you're lucky.

8: <u>Camp Four</u> You have officially entered the "death zone," so named because you're going to die up here, you damn fool. The oxygen levels are now so low that you have no choice but to start using the bottled oxygen. Don't expect this to improve your quality of life all that much.

9: <u>Summit</u> Congratulations! You're now 29,028 feet above sea level. Here's some of the exciting things you will find at the highest point on Earth.

—Gods. Many interesting deities live up here. If you see Zeus, get him to tell the one about the Athenian, the Spartan, and the Roman. It's a riot.

—The Jet Stream. These are high velocity winds that circle the Earth in East-West patterns. Right now you are standing in it, and it is trying to send you soaring into China. Don't let it, as this will also anger China.

—Clouds. That's right, you've climbed to the best lookout point on the planet and all you can see are the tops of clouds. Don't you feel foolish now?

—Satellites. There are a very large number of man-made satellites in low orbit. Make sure you duck when they pass by.

10: <u>Getting down again</u> It is very important that you get the hell off the summit right away so you can tell people. Otherwise, they won't believe you. This is what happened to George Mallory, and boy, did he feel foolish. We recommend that you climb down. In terms of speed this is not nearly as efficient as jumping, but it has a much higher survival rate.

HOW TO TELL IF YOUR HUSBAND IS IN THE MAFIA

Like alcoholism, mafia involvement is not necessarily something that a loved one will be prepared to admit to. It is therefore very important that wives or significant others recognize early the symptoms of mob-ism. It is treatable when identified early, but can become chronic if left unchecked.

(Important note: while we realize that in today's working environment, the household breadwinner is just as likely to be female as male, extensive research into mob-ism—we have seen every episode of *The Sopranos* and own all the *Godfather* movies as well as *Goodfellas* and *Miller's Crossing*—has turned up zero cases wherein the wife earned a living in the mafia and the husband did not. It would appear that mob-ism is an exclusively male condition.)

Here are some of the early signs of mafia involvement.

1: He is Italian There are a lot of Italian males in the world, and most of them will tell you that the suggestion that they are "connected" is an unfair ethnic stereotype. They say this because they don't want you to know that they are all in the mob.

2: <u>Spare cash</u> If your husband likes to keep large quantities of cash hidden throughout the house in green trash bags, this is a bad sign. White trash bags too.

3: <u>Search warrants</u> If members of the federal government like to search your home on occasion, please be advised that this is not normal, or at least not in the United States. (Exception: unless you're a Muslim.)

4: <u>Funerals</u> Do you attend a high number of funerals? One a month, say? This is fairly unusual, especially if the recently deceased all passed away as the result of an "untimely accident" involving gunshots at close range.

5: <u>Car trunk</u> Examine the contents of your husband's trunk. Look for any of the following objects: a shovel, a saw, plastic lining, a corpse. These are red flags.

6: <u>Business meetings</u> Many husbands conduct business in their homes on occasion. However, soundproofing one room of the house for these meetings is fairly unusual, as is speaking entirely in code. (Exception: your husband might actually be in the CIA, which is far worse.)

7: <u>Godfather</u> If your husband is godfather to a large number of people, most of whom you're pretty sure aren't even related to him, this is a very bad sign.

What to do

As stated above, advanced cases of mob-ism are entirely untreatable, so our advice would be to live it up while you can, as it can also be very lucrative. If you've caught it early—if, for instance, he "knows a guy who knows a guy" who's involved, and he's "got this thing" going on and "the guy" wants to know if he's "in"—there are a large number of other professions your husband might want to consider looking into before making a career choice, and many of them are legal: politician, FBI, CIA or IRS agent, gaming commissioner, talent agent, professional boxer. Be certain, in other words, that he is making an informed choice.

HOW TO STREAK DURING A MAJOR LEAGUE BASEBALL GAME

Before considering this exercise, it is wise to keep in mind a few things: it's illegal, it will NOT get you on television, and forty thousand people will get a chance to see your private parts.

1: <u>Get a seat near the field</u> Just about the only thing more ridiculous than someone running naked onto a baseball field is someone running naked through the stands in order to get to the field. If you start from the bleachers, you're probably not going to make it. Getting to the edge of the field will not be difficult if your team is not playoff-bound. Buy a cheap seat, and work your way forward over the course of the game.

2: <u>Bring a friend</u> Someone is going to have to hold your clothes for you, assuming you weren't foolish enough to come to the ball park without any.

3: <u>Get highly inebriated</u> Without the aid of copious amounts of beer it will dawn on you that this is a pretty idiotic thing to do.

4: <u>Pick your inning, and be ready for it</u> Once you have decided when to streak—most favor the late innings—be ready for a lull in action.

Since this is a baseball game, there should be hundreds of lulls per inning.

5: <u>Strip fast, and get going</u> Head for the area between the infielders and the outfielders. There is no reason to think any of the players will attempt to stop you unless doing so is part of an incentive clause in their playing contracts.

6: <u>Keep an eye peeled for ushers and policemen</u> They don't want to go anywhere near you either, because you're a naked drunk, and who wants to touch a naked drunk? They will attempt to touch you with objects that are not immediate parts of their bodies, such as billy clubs. This will hurt.

7: <u>Be sure to wave to the crowd as you're dragged off</u> You've put on quite a show. Acknowledge your fans with a wave. Use your hand.

Be aware

Very few people on this planet look attractive when completely naked, and almost none look attractive when completely naked and sprinting. So when you look at yourself in the mirror and think you're impressive, keep in mind that you are fooling yourself.

HOW TO CROSS A BUSY STREET

There are as many ways to cross a busy street as there are streets to cross. What we have tried to do is present strategies that deal with the most common types of intersections. Note: if you are from one of those states where all cars come to a screeching stop as soon as a pedestrian steps off the curb, you don't need to read this. We also recommend you never attempt to cross a street in Massachusetts, as you will be killed.

—<u>The Standard</u> This is defined as any two- or four-lane road with two-way traffic wherein a car appears approximately every three seconds, with only a median strip, no proximate stoplights, and a speed limit in excess of thirty miles per hour.

1: <u>Focus on one side</u> The way to cross this sort of street is to concentrate on only one half of the road (half is defined as "where the cars are all going in the same direction as one another.")

2: <u>Spot the gap</u> Make sure you are positioned on a straightaway that allows you to see at least two hundred yards to your left. (Or right, in England. Note: Americans should not cross streets in England.) Even with two lanes of oncoming traffic there should eventually be an opening between cars.

3: <u>Sprint</u> As soon as the opening is in front of you, run to the median strip. Do not walk casually in the hopes that once you are in the street the oncoming cars will slow down, especially since we forgot to mention to look for a crosswalk first.

4: <u>Wait for another gap</u> You should now be looking to your right. (Left, in England.) Eventually another gap should appear to allow you to sprint the remaining distance, but you must be patient as cars whiz past you on both sides, your fragile existence being protected by two thin yellow lines that are only respected in the first place because the drivers feel like it. Now is not the time to panic.

—<u>the Crossroad</u> Defined as two Standard streets crossing one another with traffic regulated by a stoplight.

1: <u>Don't be a wuss</u> Sure, usually this sort of intersection has a cross-walk, which will stop all traffic for you. And now eight lanes of people know you're a total wuss. Exceptions: small children, pregnant (third trimester only) women, persons with babies in strollers, persons with crippling physical ailments, and pregnant women with crippling physical ailments pushing a stroller and being trailed by small children.

2: <u>Identify the patterns</u> Traffic on one of the two roads will always be moving. What you want to do is identify when the cars on the road you wish to cross are not moving. This can best be determined by observing the lights. Red light is good. Green light is bad. Yellow light is very bad, as this means "drive faster" to most motorists.

3: <u>The danger zones</u> In a four lane, two-way road there are three danger zones that you have to be aware of while crossing.

> (Lanes numbered one through four from left to right)
> Lane One: Cars turning right, cars turning left against traffic.
> Lane Two: Cars turning left against traffic
> Lane Four: Cars turning right on red (where legal.)

The only safe place in the street is directly in front of a stopped car in Lane Three. It is, however, a good idea to not mock the driver of this vehicle.

—the Busy City Street This is defined as being a traffic-heavy road in the middle of a major city, at any place where pedestrians far out-number vehicles.

1: Take ownership Pedestrians rule the downtown. The sidewalk is yours, and so is the street. mob rule is in effect.

2: Step on out At every corner are loads of people just waiting for the light to change so that they may cross. They need someone to lead them. You can be that person. Take two steps out into the street and act like you don't even notice the car that's speeding toward you. (As it is, the car is probably only going about ten to fifteen miles per hour.) Once you have made the commitment to cross, you will be joined by several dozen pedestrians. The driver will stop. He may not have any qualms about hitting one single pedestrian, but he's pretty sure he'll be in trouble if he plows through a dozen.

3: The weave There are many occasions, when walking through the city, in which you will not wish to walk all the way to the corner in order to cross the street. Fortunately for you, city traffic is, by law, bumper-to-bumper twenty-four hours a day. Cars do move, but only five feet at a time. In this case, just weave between the cars. Even if a car does roll into you, the worst they can do is knock you over, and once they've done that they can't even get away because traffic is still not moving, leaving you with plenty of time to assault them.

PART IV

EMERGENCIES R US

—How to Identify and Defuse a Bomb

—How to Make Coffee After Running Out of Coffee Filters

—How to Deliver a Baby In a Manger

—How to Prepare a Human Being for Emergency Consumption

—How to Perform an Appendectomy

—How to Tell You Lost the Election

—How to Find Jesus

—How to Treat a Broken Heart

—How to Identify Anthrax

HOW TO IDENTIFY AND DEFUSE A BOMB

There are many different types of bombs and many different ways to defuse them. This list is not exhaustive. In general, it's a good idea to avoid anything ticking and anything strapped together with duct tape, especially if it's also strapped to the chest of a religious fanatic.

Types of bombs

—<u>The "black cannonball" with the lit fuse sticking out of it</u> This is the most recognizable type of bomb, and is very easy to defuse.

1: <u>Pull fuse out of bomb</u> This may not work.

2: <u>Throw bomb into large body of water</u> Small bodies of water also work quite well, but not sinks. Spitting is not terribly effective either.

"Black cannonball" bombs usually do not have a great deal of concussive force, so if you are unable to defuse it, don't worry. The worst that can happen is that you end up with tattered clothes, a blackened face, and your hair standing straight up in the air and smoking.

—<u>The time bomb</u> Time bombs can be identified by their prominently displayed timepieces, which can be either digital or analog.

1: <u>Locate the clock</u> It should be easy to find. As a rule, there will not be enough time on it for you to get an expert to defuse it for you.

2: <u>Find the wires</u> All time bombs have wires coming out of the timer, and the wires are always different colors. There are usually two wires, but some have three.

3: <u>Prepare to cut one</u> This will be the wrong wire. Do not actually cut it, but it's important to make the bomb think you are going to cut it.

4: <u>Pick a different wire</u> It doesn't matter which one.

5: <u>Say something pithy</u> "Here goes nothing" is fairly standard. Also, "I hope this works."

6: <u>Pause dramatically, and then cut the wire</u> Do not exhale for several seconds. The clock may stop ticking, but it doesn't have to.

—<u>The radio-controlled bomb</u> These are very similar to time bombs in that should you find an opportunity to locate the actual bomb, you can defuse it by cutting a colored wire at random. Often, however, this is not an option.

1: <u>Locate the person with the radio-controller</u> He is usually an evil terrorist of some sort. If you cannot find him quickly, you may want to ask around. ("Hello, are you an evil terrorist?")

2: <u>Beat him up</u> This is the quickest way to get the remote device. Shooting him can also be very effective.

—<u>The nuclear bomb</u> These simply don't explode, but since everyone gets all worried about the threat of them going off, it's best to respect them nonetheless.

1: <u>Find out who has the bomb and what they want</u> Usually, they have very reasonable demands, i.e., getting missiles out of Cuba. Try and meet these demands if possible.

2: <u>Claim to have bombs of your own</u> They don't know if you really have a bomb any more than you really know if they have a bomb. With luck, they will spend all their money trying to have more bombs than you do, and not have enough left over to actually launch the bombs in your direction.

—<u>The cinematic bomb</u> These are characterized by extremely poor newspaper reviews consisting of one star or fewer. While extremely dangerous, they defuse themselves within a week or two, although they can resurface later on videotape.

HOW TO MAKE COFFEE AFTER RUNNING OUT OF COFFEE FILTERS

1: <u>Don't panic</u> Most injuries related to lack of coffee consumption result from semi-conscious hysteria.

2: <u>Find a napkin, a paper towel, or a sock</u> An ordinary four-folded nakpin is ideal. If there are no paper products are available, a sock will do. If no clean socks are available, remove one of the ones from your feet. Just don't tell anyone.

3: <u>Place the napkin, paper towel, or sock into the basket</u> The napkin should be unfolded so that its corners stick out of the basket.

4: <u>Add coffee grounds</u> Once grounds have been placed inside the napkin or paper towel, fold the corners over the top. With the sock, just make sure the grounds go all the way to the toe.

5: <u>Add extra water</u> Napkins, towels and socks are more absorbent than coffee filters. Add an extra half-cup or so of water.

Things to know

—Generally speaking, it is probably not a good idea to say anything when someone says "hey, this coffee tastes like feet!" Try to be near the coffee machine when it has finished brewing so that you can remove your sock before anyone sees.

—Chewing coffee grounds in lieu of brewing coffee doesn't work very well, and you will never get the grounds out of your teeth. Snorting coffee grounds works somewhat better, but you may never be able to smell anything but coffee for the remainder of your life.

HOW TO DELIVER A BABY IN A MANGER

Statistically speaking, more babies have been born in mangers during the month of December than in any other month in the year, so it is wise to be prepared for this possibility, even if you do not live near Bethlehem, or other manger-populous locales. Keep this in mind.

Delivering a baby in a manger is very similar in most aspects to delivering a baby in a taxicab or hospital, insofar as a newborn infant at some point emerges from a human female. However, the likely deification of said newborn can tend to complicate matters.

1: <u>Determine if the mother is ready</u> The easiest way to ascertain this is to check the current date. If it is December 25, now is probably the time. Otherwise, this may be a false alarm.

2: <u>Clear a space</u> Unfortunately, the manger will soon be very crowded with sheep, cows, shepherds, wise men, drummer boys, and seraphim. Recommend that they come back later. Be firm.

3: <u>Obtain swaddling clothes</u> Someone there should know what the hell swaddling clothes are. Get some.

4: <u>Check for the baby's head</u> This should be quite simple, because of the halo, which will be providing ample illumination. Open the mother's legs and peer inside. If you are bathed in heavenly glow, the head is ready to crown. (Note: be careful not to confuse the heavenly glow from the newborn halo with the halos of the mother or the surrogate father. Likewise, the large star overhead may throw you off.)

5: <u>Get ready to catch it</u> You will not have to help ease the baby from his mother all that much, but it would probably be a bad idea to just let him plop out on the floor of the manger.

6: <u>Wrap him up and put him down</u> Once the baby has emerged, wrap him up in the swaddling clothes and put him in a bed of straw. The good news here is that you don't even have to worry about an afterbirth, since he comes with a belly button. If you do this well, he may even bless you.

7: <u>Notify</u> Inform the nearest seraphim that it's a boy savior, so that it can fly around the countryside telling important persons about it, like shepherds, and Harold the angel.

Things to know

Successfully delivering a baby in a manger automatically qualifies you for sainthood. Contact your local Catholic church for details and the proper application forms.

HOW TO PREPARE A HUMAN BEING FOR EMERGENCY CONSUMPTION

The most common complaints of survivors who had to resort to cannibalism is that their fellow humans tasted "sort of gamey." With the proper preparation this culinary disaster can be averted.

(Note: this is for emergencies only, such as being unexpectedly stranded on a desert island, a raft in the middle of the ocean, or the side of a snow-capped mountain. Just being very hungry is not considered an emergency.)

1: <u>Make sure the human is dead</u> In most circumstances, your erstwihile meal has perished on his or her own due to natural or accidental causes. However, in the event that this is not the case—if for instance, lots have been drawn—it may be necessary to slay your dinner yourself. It would be unwise to simply fly into a murderous rage and start whacking him or her with whatever is available, as this might do damage to important body parts that will subsequently be much more difficult to properly prepare for consumption. Severe head wounds, strangulation or other forms of suffocation such as drowning, or general head removal, are all viable options.

2: <u>Prepare your meal</u> Arms, legs and buttocks tend to have the most useful meat, although if you've been isolated for a long time, this may not necessarily be the case. Fortunately, many internal organs are edible and quite tasty, even though they tend to be somewhat gross looking. We recommend the kidneys, the liver, and the heart. The stomach should be avoided, as should the intestinal tract. The lungs will unfortunately have very little meat.

Separate the arms and legs from the torso using whatever sharp implement is available. (If no knives are handy, the human can be drawn and quartered with the help of three friends and a little effort.) Open the chest cavity by prying off the ribcage. Be sure to save the ribs if possible, as they will have plenty of meat on them as well.

3: <u>Build a fire</u> Please don't eat the human raw. Frankly, that's just disgusting. Arms and legs should be held over the fire no longer than ten minutes, while internal organs should cook for at least twenty. Most survival kits contain a small supply of table salt, cayenne pepper, and oregano. Season generously. Be sure to baste occasionally with whatever water supply is available to keep the meat from drying up. (Important note: when basting with salt water, be sure to reduce cooking salt accordingly.)

4: <u>Dig in!</u> Use additional seasonings where necessary.

HOW TO PERFORM AN APPENDECTOMY

Use this procedure only when you are absolutely certain that the person in question actually has appendicitis. Appendicitis can be chacterized as a sharp pain somewhere on the lower right portion of the torso. The pain should be sharp enough that the person says "oww, I think I have appendicitis." If they say "oww, I think I have gas," this is a good indication that they only have gas. It is probably also a good idea to call an ambulance before proceeding.

You will need: A sharp knife, a pair of scissors, a smock or apron or clothes you don't care too much about, and help from a couple of strong people.

1: <u>Lie the person down flat on the ground</u> As there is no anaesthesia available in most cases, and as this is a very painful procedure, make sure the strong people you have brought with you hold your patient down.

2: <u>Make one north-south incision starting at the bottom of the rib-cage and stopping above the hip</u> This will have to be very deep in order to penetrate the outer muscle layer to expose the internal organs. In the event you have laid your patient down with their head to the south and not the north, make the incision south to north instead. Do not lie the patient east-west or you will confuse everything.

3: <u>Fight the gag reflex</u> Internal organs are really icky and plus, there's bound to be a lot of blood by now. Resist the urge to lose your lunch, as this could result in a dangerous infection.

4: <u>Find the appendix</u> Nobody really knows where the appendix is, so you're going to have to poke around for a bit. The patient's assistance is critical here. Lightly touch random internal organs, asking each time "does this hurt?" If the patient says yes, that's probably the appendix.

5: <u>Remove the appendix</u> Use the scissors to cut the appendix loose. It should be fairly small. IMPORTANT: If it is beating steadily, it is not the appendix; it is the heart. Do not remove it. Instead, review direction number two, as you have made your incision in the wrong place altogether.

6: <u>Apply direct pressure</u> Try and close the incision as well as you can and then apply direct pressure to it so that it closes up. The paramedics will take care of the rest.

HOW TO TELL YOU'VE LOST THE ELECTION

Before proceeding, it is important that we grasp exactly what an "election" is.

There are many different ways to determine who the leader of a country (or state, town, city, coven, group, council, etc.) will be.

—Representative model This is by far the most common method. The persons who are in need of governing decide, in a somewhat orderly fashion, who they would like to make decisions for them. Their vote is informed by "campaign advertisements," which are designed to reveal who it is bad to vote for. Their goal is to choose the lesser of two evils. Note: in many cases, the persons elected into office subsequently vote for their own leader as well, and so on, and so on. This is what is known as "bureaucracy." It is this model which we will focus on in this chapter.

—Dictatorship model Far less common today, this method relies on the decision-making abilities of large military forces. These forces "vote" by agreeing who to follow, and then they kill anyone who doesn't agree with them. Dictatorships can be very unstable; leaders are chosen by coup, and most are unscheduled. Thus, leaders may have a very high turnover (such as in most Czech republics) or have an uncommonly long term of service (Cuba.)

—<u>Appointment model</u> In this version, leaders are voted upon by a committee of sub-leaders, in a fashion similar to the "bureaucracy" approach. However, the voters that comprise the committee are not themselves elected into office, but appointed by prior leaders. This arrangement is often confused with the communist method in places such as China and the old Soviet Union. It is also employed with great success in the Vatican City.

—<u>Communist method</u> True communism has no leaders. Every decision is made by every person within the system. This is why the only true communists are wandering around looking for someone to tell them what to do, and why there are no large-scale, functioning communist societies today.

—<u>Heirarchal method</u> There is no electoral process involved. The leader is born into his or her position and is referred to as "king" or "queen." On rare occasions, the leader is chosen by a magic sword stuck in a large rock. There are very few heirarchies left, but there are many virtual heirarchies, such as the Kennedys.

—<u>Darwinian method</u> The leader in this sort of society is whoever is the biggest and strongest. He is referred to as the "Alpha male." While many of the elements of the Darwinian method can be found in both the dictatorship and representative models, pure forms are very rare, existing mainly in primitive cultures, non-human primate groups, professional sports, and Arnold Schwarzenegger films.

As we can see, actual elections—where the entire governed body chooses a leader—exist in only one model.

1: <u>Counting the vote</u> At the conclusion of the electoral process, all of the votes that have been cast are actually counted by somebody. If it turns out you have fewer votes than even one of your opponents, you have probably not won the election. "Counting" is a mathematical process also referred to formally as "addition." Numbers are "added" together until there are no more numbers left. Mathematicians agree that the process of "addition" is unaffected by when the math is done or who is doing it. Thus, if you find yourself arguing that two plus two does not equal four if it is added together next week by a person with a particular political affiliation, you are just grasping at straws.

2: <u>What is a vote?</u> A vote is a decision made by a single voter in favor of a single candidate. In most cases, each person gets only one vote, although there are exceptions. If, in the process of gaining political office, you find it necessary to redefine the definition of a "vote," this is a very strong indication that you may have lost.

3: <u>You find yourself in court</u> If you need a judge to decide if you won, you probably lost, no matter how many thousands of lawyers you've brought with you. And taking it to the Supreme court doesn't look real good either.

4: <u>You hire Alan Dershowitz</u> His resume includes Klaus Von Bulow, O.J. Simpson, and Mike Tyson. Hiring him simply does not make you look good. You have probably lost.

5: <u>You are a third party candidate</u> The vast majority of the country in which you live consists of moderate individuals with moderate views. If you are a candidate who appeals only to fringe individuals possessed of extreme views, then by definition, you are courting the minority. As we have seen in rule number two, each one of your supporters only has one vote, and as we have seen in rule number one, the rules of "addition" aren't changing any time soon. If, on the other hand, you are a third party candidate with moderate views that might appeal to moderate individuals, you will still be viewed as the guy neither major party wanted. We recommend moving to a country where the dictatorship model is still in effect.

6: <u>Changing the law of the land</u> If, in order to gain the office you desire, you must first subvert the entire electoral process by breaking the law, you have probably already lost. This includes asking your brother to change the law for you. As before, you may want to consider moving to a country that honors the dictatorship method.

7: <u>You refuse to concede</u> Being the last person in the country to agree on who won the election looks exceptionally bad if you are one of the ones that did not win. Covering your ears and going "LA-LA-LA-LA-I-CAN'T-HEAR-YOU" whenever someone points out that you lost also does not look good.

As you can see, what sounds like a fairly simple process can occasionally get very complicated. As an example, according to the above guide none of the 2000 Presidential candidates in the United States actually won the election.

What to do

—You can continue to run every four years for the same office, looking more and more pitiful every year. This approach is favored by most third-party candidates and also Hubert Humphrey.

—You can win the office at some point in the future, only to bring great shame to yourself, your party, your job, and your country because you have become bitter, acrimonious, and paranoid. This is also known as the Nixon method.

—You can retire from public service and become an elder statesman, reappearing only occasionally to build a house, negotiate a peace settlement, or discuss an embarrassing medical problem.

—You can try and get your oldest son elected instead.

HOW TO FIND JESUS

Finding Jesus can be critically important in an emergency. The key is knowing where to look.

1: <u>Don't panic</u> Many people, after realizing they have lost Jesus, become panicky. This can be very dangerous. Instead, take a few deep breaths, relax, and think: where was the last place you had Jesus? Go there.

2: <u>Look around</u> Be thorough. Did you look behind the couch? He might be there. Don't just glance around the room, either. Lift things up. He might be in the clothing hamper, for instance. Check there. He's probably right where you left Him.

3: <u>Ask around</u> If you still cannot find Jesus, talk to others. Do not ask them "have you found Jesus?" For one thing, they may have never misplaced him in the first place, so your question might be construed as awkward. Also, you might not want to admit you've lost Him, as this is a reasonably irresponsible thing to do. Instead, ask if they've seen Him recently, and if so, where. Here is a list of people who might know where Jesus is:

—Professional athletes. They are finding Jesus on a daily basis, because He is a big sports fan.

—Clergymen. Priests, monks, pastors, rectors, elders, and chaplains are all good people to talk to about this. You may find that many of them haven't seen Jesus in a long time, but they are usually pretty good at finding Him in a pinch.

—The Pope. The upside is that not only does he know where to find Jesus, he probably had lunch with Him yesterday. The downside is that the Pope's schedule is usually very full.

4: <u>Bounty hunters</u> If you are still unable to find Jesus, you may want to consider this option, although it is somewhat extreme and not likely to work. Bounty hunters are people who will find Jesus for you, but you have to pay them. They usually dress in white clothing for some reason, many are from the South, and all of them spend a lot of time on television announcing their desire to help you find Jesus, provided you send them cash. Dealing with a bounty hunter is a lot like speaking to a used car salesman. If you ask "how much will it cost to find Jesus?" they may quote a price, but that is not the final price, and next week they are charging you double. If you are not careful, before long you will have sent them all of your money, and they still have not found Jesus for you. Then they will claim that this is your fault. The truth is, they either don't know where to find Jesus, or they mistook someone else for Him.

Things to know

—Once you have found Jesus, keep an eye on him. He may wander off again.

—In the event that you never find Jesus, consider the possibility that He does not want you to find Him.

HOW TO TREAT A BROKEN HEART

The heart is one of the most important organs in the human body, so it is critical that a broken one is treated immediately, before irreversible damage is done to the cardiopulmonary system. You must be prepared to recognize the symptoms, which include:

—uncontrollable weeping at totally inappropriate moments
—random acts of violence, such as throwing objects and starting wars
—poor grooming habits
—homelessness
—large amounts of free time
—awkward sexual advances

It is a little-known medical fact that males and females have different hearts, and so, require different care. We offer both treatments.

Male

1: <u>Get him drunk</u> Take him to a bar, and get him completely messed up. This can be very expensive, but is now covered by most comprehensive health care providers. Be sure to keep a receipt.

2: <u>Communicate</u> This consists mostly of grunting "bitch" every few minutes while patting him on the back. Later, you may wish to add "you're better off without her" or "she was ugly anyway."

3: <u>Get him some sex</u> In the event that he is unattractive, you may have to pay for someone to have sex with him. This is also covered by most comprehensive health care providers.

4: <u>Repeat</u> Follow steps one through three until the broken heart has been mended, or until he has joined Alcoholics Anonymous.

Female

1: <u>Binge</u> You will need to obtain a lot of chocolate, as well as ice cream and cookie dough.

2: <u>Communicate</u> She will want to describe everything that went wrong with the relationship, and she will begin at the very beginning, by which we mean, starting with when homo sapiens first crafted primitive stone tools. This could take several days. You are not required to speak, an in fact, it is not recommended. Instead, nod emphatically on occasion, go "Uh!" every now and then, and once an hour, roll your eyes and look exasperated. Maintain eye contact on a fairly regular basis and you will not even need to actually listen to what she is saying.

3: <u>Rent movies</u> An important part of the mending process is making the female cry a lot. Before films, this was done by pinching, or poking with sharp objects, but now these techniques are no longer necessary. You will have to rent romantic movies, such as *Sleepless in Seattle* or *When Harry Met Sally*. (Just about any movie starring Meg Ryan will work, except for *Joe Versus the Volcano*, which is not fit to be witnessed by human beings, and was actually made primarily to entertain squirrel monkeys and small marsupials.) The romantic film will provide her with imaginary happy ending scenarios that will make her feel worse because she didn't get that happy ending, which will make her cry, which will in turn make her feel better. Nobody knows why this is.

4: <u>Repeat</u> Continue steps one through three—and especially step two—until either the heart has mended or she has eaten so much cookie dough she can no longer leave her home.

Things to know

—Consoling a friend who has a broken heart and is also a member of the opposite sex is a great way to get laid, provided you are a heterosexual.

—If you are friends with both parties, your best bet is to change your phone number, your job, and your residence immediately. Trust us.

HOW TO IDENTIFY
ANTHRAX

Anthrax is a disease caused by the bacterium *bacillus anthracis* and named after a heavy metal band from the Eighties. Since anthrax can cause many adverse effects that will kill you, it is important to know how to recognize it, how the disease manifests itself, and what to do if you think you have it.

<u>Identifying and Avoiding Anthrax</u>

Most doctors agree that the best way to avoid anthrax is by not coming into contact with *bacillus anthracis*. Therefore do not go near any of the following:

—Dead livestock
—Livestock that isn't dead yet
—White powder in envelopes
—White powder not in envelopes
—The film *Powder*
—Envelopes in general
—Mailboxes, post offices, or mail carriers
—Congress
—Reporters for a daily metropolitan newspaper (exception: Superman)
—Crop dusters

—Crops
—Dusters
—Dust

If you believe you have discovered *bacillus anthracis,* contact your local authorities immediately. Be sure to scream a lot and exaggerate if necessary. Remember, it is their responsibility to respond to every single report, and they are glad to do it because they are not all that busy.

<u>Do I Have Anthrax?</u>

Before identifying the symptoms to see if you have anthrax, take the following quiz.

Are you:

…a person who is theoretically important enough for someone to actually say "I would like to give this person a fatal disease?" If no, you probably do not have anthrax.

…a member of the press or a government employee? If no, you probably do not have anthrax.

…a farmer? If no, you probably do not have anthrax.

…a hypochondriac? Yeah, like you're going to listen to us one way or another.

<u>Disease Symptoms and What To Do If You Have Them</u>

There are three ways to contract anthrax: inhalation, cutaneous contact, and ingestion. A fourth method, abject hysteria, has not yet been medically proven.

Inhalation

By far the most dangerous of the three infection methods, its can be identified by flu-like symptoms, followed by immediate death. If you think you may have inhaled anthrax—say, for instance, you had flu-like symptoms yesterday and are dead today—the wisest recourse may be to take the antibiotic Cipro immediately, prior to formal diagnosis. If you do not have easy access to Cipro, just take whatever antibiotic you can find. Don't worry about possibly creating antibiotic resistance in whatever other diseases you happen to be carrying around; they'll just have to invent new antibiotics for them.

Cutaneous Contact

This means you've touched, pet, or fondled anthrax. It is identified by a mild rash, followed by a bump similar to a bug bite, followed by flu-like symptoms, followed by death. Cutaneous contact is not nearly as lethal as inhalation, but it itches like a bastard. The wisest recourse is take Cipro if you itch anywhere.

Ingestion

If you are eating anthrax, there may already be something wrong with you. We cannot recall a single instance of someone saying "you know what this gravy needs? Anthrax." It is not a food supplement. It also adds little flavor to gravy. We recommend a little salt, and maybe a touch of worcestershire sauce to give it some zing. Symptoms include stomach pains, mild diarhhea, flu-like symptoms, and death. Take Cipro, and an antacid.

Things To Know

—Anthrax is not contagious, but we'd still like it if you didn't come near us
—Seriously, stay the hell away
—There are a couple of generic antibiotics that have proven to be as

effective as Cipro in combating anthrax. However, the FDA has formally approved only Cipro for treatment, and the FDA is an adjunct of the U.S. government, and we trust the U.S. government this week. In the event that you cannot get Cipro because supplies are low and Bayer is still refusing to allow generic versions to be manufactured, you may have no option but to die. This is known as the American Way.

PART V

❀

SURVIVING WHEN YOU SHOULD REALLY JUST DIE

—How to Live Through the Sinking of an Ocean Liner That Has Struck an Iceberg

—How to Survive a Trip to Disney World

—How to Survive On the Moon

—How to Avoid Getting Struck By Lightning

—How to Determine If Your Neighbor is a Serial Killer

—How to Take a Bullet

—How to Survive a U.S. Bombing Raid

HOW TO LIVE THROUGH THE SINKING OF AN OCEAN LINER THAT HAS STRUCK AN ICEBERG

1: <u>Locate the nearest lifeboat</u> There will not be enough, so act fast!

2: <u>Be a woman or a child</u> In today's world, almost without exception, it pays to be an adult male. This is not one of those times. When electing to be a woman or a child, it will also be to your benefit to be a first class passenger. If you cannot be a woman or a child, please continue reading the directions, below, although frankly, your chances don't look so good.

3: <u>Do NOT befriend a large-breasted redhead</u> For starters, she won't get on the damn lifeboat even though she fits the minimum requirement of being either a woman or a child. Also, if you end up in the water with her, she'll take up all the space on the driftwood, leaving you treading water. This could be fatal.

4: <u>Locate the part of the ship that is sinking, and get as far away from it as you can</u>

5: <u>Stay out of the water as long as possible</u> You will probably fall comically to your death when the ship turns completely sideways and raises your end into the air by eighty feet. But at least you didn't drown.

6: <u>Start swimming</u> In the unlikely event that you are not dead already, as soon as the ship goes underwater you will be underwater as well, which makes this a very good time to start swimming.

7: <u>Find something that is floating, and hold onto it</u> Driftwood, a life-jacket (even one still attached to a person,) or an island will do.

8: <u>Wait for someone to rescue you</u> If nobody does, sorry. We're actually surprised you made it this far.

Things to know

While massive ocean liners rarely strike icebergs any more, it is always wise to treat icebergs with respect, as they can be very danger-ous when provoked.

HOW TO SURVIVE A TRIP TO DISNEY WORLD

Disney World is one of the harshest, most unforgiving environments on the face of the Earth. It is also one of the few places on Earth where safety in numbers does not apply. Here, the larger your group is, the more unlikely survival becomes, especially if children are involved.

1: <u>Check your funds</u> Carefully review your currency and credit cards, including taking note of your available credit limits. Do this before you are on Disney property, at the airport.

2: <u>Just say no</u> You will have to practice this a good deal, especially if you are traveling with children. Start at the hotel lobby. When you check in the kindly—and cleverly disguised—alien being working the front desk will ask you if you wish to link your room key to your credit card, so that all you need to do to buy things is hand over your room key. This is like loaning your house keys to the Manson family. You must say no. They will even ask if you wish to link your childrens' room keys to your credit card so that they can purchase things without first acquiring your approval. We really shouldn't have to tell you what an incredibly bad idea this is.

3: <u>Avoiding the parks</u> This is impossible, but it makes us feel better to suggest it anyhow.

4: <u>Beating the heat</u> Disney World is maintained at the constant temperature of 92 degrees, and humidity is shipped in from the Amazon. This is done to wear down your decision-making abilities and make it seem as if a $5-bottle of water and a cheap plastic pocket fan are good investments. Also, the only air conditioning available other than your hotel room is in the shops. There are five shops on average to every ride at Disney World. And your hotel air conditioning is designed to turn off if you remain in your room for more than ten hours consecutively. Buy one bottle of water per family member, and keep refilling them at water fountains, or in your room every morning. Don't bother with the cheap plastic fans.

5: <u>Complain loudly</u> Do not make the mistake of assuming that just because you don't see an enormous line, there isn't one hidden somewhere. Some lines run underground for seven miles. Your best bet is to be a total jerk. Wait until you are in earshot of a friendly Disney employee and then start bitching. The louder and more graphic you are, the better. (Warn your children in advance that they are about to learn some new words they should not repeat.) Disney employees do not know what unhappiness and dissatisfaction is, because these things do not exist on their planet. Confronted with this problem, they will take you through a side door that leads to the front of the line.

6: <u>The wheelchair</u> If complaining loudly does not work (or your vocabulary is inadequate) travel with a wheelchair. This will also get you right to the front of the line. If you are lucky, you already have a crippled person with you. Otherwise, one of your family members will have to pretend to be handicapped. Make it a game and take turns.

7: <u>Do not buy anything</u> We mean it. It will start small, with a pair of Mickey Mouse ears or a stuffed animal or something, and before you know it, you're taking home a framed cel autographed by the guy who did the character's voice that will serve you no purpose other than reminding you where your mortgage money went. This will require a great deal of discipline, because everything there is for sale, including the employees. Especially avoid Downtown Disney and the World Showcase at Epcot.

8: <u>Do not go on Test Track</u> It sucks.

9: <u>Flee from the characters</u> Often, you will sit down to eat and find yourself unexpectedly assaulted by employees in character suits. Do not let them get near your children. While you get your camera out, they will whisper things in your child's ear like "if your mommy and daddy don't buy more toys for you, we will have to kill them" or "if they don't give you everything you want, they don't love you."

10: <u>Bring Disney paraphernalia with you</u> You have undoubtedly invested heavily in Disney merchandise before having made this trip. Take it with you. When you leave, they will search your bags to be certain you have made enough purchases. Your pre-purchased products should throw them off.

HOW TO SURVIVE ON THE MOON

Finding oneself stranded on the moon for any length of time can be perilous indeed. Since the moon has no atmosphere, breathing is highly unlikely. The dark side of the moon is extraordinarily cold. On the sunny side, since there is no ozone layer, the sun, while keeping you warm, will fry you with unblocked ultraviolet radiation. Your focus should be on getting the hell off the moon as soon as you possibly can. This is not a place to camp out overnight.

You will need:

—A functional space suit
—A large supply of oxygen in sealed containers

(Note: both items are difficult to obtain. Shop around. We recommend always keeping your suit and oxygen tanks in the trunk of your car, so that you can gain quick access to them in the lunar environment. Also please note, an internal combustion engine will not function on the moon.)

1: <u>Get your bearings</u> Look around. The entire surface of the moon is littered with rocks and dust, and essentially bereft of noticeable landmarks when not viewed from orbit. So don't look there. Instead, look up. Try to locate the Earth. The Earth is a large, non-glowing, marble-like orb of varying blue, brown, and white. If what you are looking at is bright orange and glowing intensely, you are not looking at the Earth, you are looking at the Sun. And you are now blind.

2: Signal The goal here is to get the attention of someone on Earth, so that they can drive the shuttle over and pick you up. Tragically, a signal flare is of no use to you on the moon. Likewise, jumping up and down and waving your arms will not only fail, it will likely send you into low orbit. Instead, locate a reflective object, such as a mirror. In a pinch, the visor on your helmet will do. Try to reflect the sunlight (again: do NOT look at the sun directly) toward the Earth. With any luck, a bored astronomer will see your signal.

3: Make a sign Try and form a brief sign out of local rocks. The sign should identify you as being in need of immediate rescue: "HELP" if you have very few rocks, "HELP, I AM STRANDED ON THE MOON" if rocks are plentiful. Do not get cute and arrange the rocks into the shape of a face. Someone tried this on Mars once, and not only are people still talking about it, nobody got rescued.

4: Stay put Try not to stray too far from your signalling point, unless you see a strong reason to. Good reasons include: finding the entrance to the lair of a lonely mad scientist, discovering the secret NASA facility where experiments continue to this day to come up with a new product to compete with Tang, getting seized by space aliens, finding the lunar lander from 1968, which may still have some food on it.

5: Sleep a lot It may be a long wait before the shuttle shows up to get you back home, so lack of oxygen is going to be an issue fairly quickly. A sleeping person needs roughly 1/3 of the oxygen a non-sleeping person needs, so take a lot of naps. Don't worry about missing the shuttle; the sign you made out of rocks should get their attention.

HOW TO AVOID GETTING STRUCK BY LIGHTNING

Annually, lightning kills more people than shark attacks, contaminated meat products, and Sandinistan Guerillas combined. Lightning has even killed sharks eating contaminated Sandinistan Guerillas.

1: <u>Don't go out</u> It will be very difficult for lightning to find you if you live in your basement. This, however, is very impractical.

2: <u>Try not to be evil</u> It is well-known that lightning almost always strikes evil people. Strive to not be evil, and avoid blasphemy if at all possible. *(See, "How To Get Into Heaven")*

3: <u>Do not hold onto long metal objects during thunderstorms while standing on a hill</u> This is just good advice in general, unless you are a golfer.

4: <u>Listen for it</u> Unfortunately, sound does not travel as fast as light does, so you cannot be expected to react effectively in dodging the lightning by listening for the unmistakable sound of a thunderclap. However, the air will crackle just milliseconds before a lightning strike. When you hear that sound, jump out of the way real fast.

HOW TO TELL IF YOUR NEIGHBOR IS A SERIAL KILLER

1: <u>He's a nice guy you would never suspect of doing such a thing</u> Serial killers are always described by neighbors as being "such a nice guy" and "very quiet, not the sort of person you would expect to do something like this." Had these neighbors known this is exactly what they should be looking for, many lives would have been saved.

2: <u>He's a white male living alone</u> Despite many NAACP and Civil Liberties Union protests, 99% of serial killer jobs in the United States are filled by white males with poor social skills. Several court orders have done little to curb this disgraceful hiring practice.

3: <u>Late night gardening</u> It is highly uncommon for people to tend their garden in the middle of the night. In the event that you observe your neighbor digging in the back yard well after sunset, take this under consideration, especially if he does not actually maintain a garden, i.e., there don't appear to be any flowers or food products being tended. Likewise, if he's digging in the winter, this is bad.

4: <u>Garbage day</u> Keep an eye out for large trash bags in the shape of human beings. This is fairly unusual.

5: <u>Missing people</u> You must be especially observant of your neighborhood. Take note of sudden absences. Check your milk cartons regularly to confirm that you do not know any of the people on them. And if you have a different mailman every week, this is a very bad sign.

6: <u>Listen carefully</u> High-pitched shrieks are reasonably uncommon, even in today's cities. If you hear loud human-like shouts coming from your neighbor's home, take note. If the shrieking suddenly stops, take note of this as well. Exception: if your neighbor has a baby, don't worry; this is a normal sound.

7: <u>Strike up a conversation</u> Sometimes the direct approach is the best. Here are some talking points to consider.

—"So, what do you do for a living?" (If his response is either "I kill people" or "I work for the Postal Service," run. If he says "I'm an IRS agent," run from this as well, but for a different reason entirely.)
—"I'm thinking of buying an industrial-sized freezer. Do you recommend any particular brand?"
—"What is your favorite song off of the Beatles' White Album?"
—"I love dogs. Sometimes it seems like they can almost talk."
—"So what made you decide to shave half your head like that?"
—"Have you ever wondered what people taste like?"
—"Your lawn looks great! What sort of fertilizer do you use?"
—"Hey, cool van. How come you blacked out all the windows?"
—"Can I borrow a band saw?"

What to do

If you have determined that your neighbor is a serial killer, you are in a tremendous amount of trouble, because after all those questions he probably realizes you're on to him. You could call the police, but there is a good chance they won't believe you, so you're probably better off just moving immediately. No, I mean now. Forget your stuff. Really, get the hell out.

HOW TO TAKE A BULLET

1: <u>Fall down</u> Even though the bullet is simply not big enough to knock down a person no matter how fast it's going, you are supposed to fall down. Nobody knows why this is, but it looks good on film, so go with it.

2: <u>Determine where you've been hit</u> This is usually the part of your body that is bleeding that wasn't bleeding earlier.

3: <u>Apply direct pressure to the wound, while flailing about and screaming</u> Clutching the wound and acting as if you are in tremendous agony is the universal symbol for "please assist me, as I have been shot." Cursing is optional.

4: <u>Shoot back</u> Draw your own weapon and shoot at the person who shot you in the first place. Coordinating this with direction number three (above) is very difficult and will require practice. IMPORTANT: Do not follow this direction if you have shot yourself.

Things to know

—Generally speaking, bullet wounds to the head and heart tend to be fatal. Try to avoid these sorts of wounds if at all possible by ducking, or catching the bullet with your hand.

—Do not attempt to catch bullets with your teeth.

—Do not attempt to halt bullets in midair with your latent telekinetic abilities because this would be a bad way to find out you have
no latent telekinetic abilities.

HOW TO LIVE THROUGH A U.S. BOMBING RAID

Before discussing the best way to survive a U.S. bombing raid, it may be wise to determine whether or not you are a candidate for one. Otherwise, you may just be getting worried over nothing.

—Have you recently done something to make the United States very very angry? We do not mean "raise tariffs" angry, we mean "kill lots of Americans" angry or "invade countries that are selling us oil" angry. If yes, please continue.

—Are you the leader of a sovereign nation? If no, you definitely have a problem. Please continue. If yes, you might be okay, because the U.S. has a law prohibiting the assassination of foreign leaders. Unfortunately, this law is subject to change without notice, so please continue.

—Do you currently reside on U.S. soil? If yes, in all likelihood bombing will not be the method employed to apprehend you, as you may be standing near other Americans at the time, and U.S. bombs are not currently that accurate. (This is also subject to change without notice.) If no, this means the United States needs to go and get you somehow, and bombs are a pretty good way to do that, especially if you reside in a country that does not intend to hand you over.

How to Survive

1: <u>Get underground</u> Heavily fortified underground bunkers are definitely the way to go here, but these are unfortunately somewhat rare. Your best bet is to find a cave of some kind. If this is also not available, you're pretty screwed, because a foxhole just isn't going to cut it.

2: <u>Keep moving</u> The United States has an awful lot of bombs lying around, and a large number of planes with which to deliver them, but there are still going to be times over the course of the day when nobody is dropping any bombs. Depending on how angry you have gotten the U.S., we may be talking about a half hour tops here but still, when the opportunity arises, move to a different location.

3: <u>Don't push your luck</u> You will have plenty of time to spare while sitting in your underground hiding place and waiting for the massive barrage of explosions to subside. Do not spend that time making home movies no matter how bored you are. And if you must make home movies, avoid saying anything like "neener-neener" and "you ca-an't catch me, la-la-la-la-la-la." And if you do say something like this on camera, destroy the tape immediately. Do not submit it to a network for future broadcasting. Really, this is just asking for it.

4: <u>Look for American soldiers</u> If you live long enough, eventually a U.S. soldier or two will walk by. Their job is to find out if there is anything left to bomb and to look for loose change. Oh, and to kill you and anyone you may be with. Do not shoot at them. This is extremely important. Instead, throw down your gun and surrender immediately. They may still kill you and everyone you're with, but it's worth a shot, and it will definitely end the bombing.

Things to know

—If you are seriously considering angering the United States enough to inspire them to bomb you, there may be something very wrong with you psychologically. We recommend that you seek counseling, as there are a wide range of psychotropic drugs available now that can give you the same satisfaction as angering the United States without the messy side effects.

0-595-26152-3

Printed in the United States
35910LVS00005B/271-273